THE POETS'
GRIMM

20ᵗʰ Cent

Grimm Fa y ules

THE POETS' GRIMM

20th Century Poems from Grimm Fairy Tales

Edited by

JEANNE MARIE BEAUMONT

CLAUDIA CARLSON

Story Line Press
2003

For my students, who knew who Rapunzel was.
—JMB

For my daughters, Natalie and Caitlin Allen;
these stories are yours to tell.
—CSC

Copyright © 2003 by Jeanne Marie Beaumont and Claudia Carlson.
FIRST PRINTING

Published by STORY LINE PRESS, Three Oaks Farm, PO Box 1240, Ashland, OR 97520-0055, www.storylinepress.com.

This publication was made possible thanks in part to the generous support of the Nicholas Roerich Museum, the Andrew W. Mellon Foundation and our individual contributors.

The text of this book was set in Fairfield and the display type is Gill Sans.
Book designed by Claudia Carlson.
Cover art by Kay Nielsen, from the 1925 edition of *Hansel and Gretel and Other Stories by the Brothers Grimm*, reproduced by permission of Hodder and Stoughton Publishers.
Acknowledgments begin on page 273.

LIBRARY OF CONGRESS CATALOGING-IN-PUBLICATION DATA
The poets' Grimm : 20th century poems from Grimm fairy tales / edited by Jeanne Marie Beaumont, Claudia Carlson.
       p. cm.
   Includes bibliographical references and index.
   ISBN 1-58654-027-0
1. Fairy tales—Adaptations. 2. Grimm, Jacob, 1785-1863—Adaptations.
3. Grimm, Wilhelm, 1786-1859—Adaptations. 4. American poetry—
20th century. 5. Folklore—Poetry.
I. Beaumont, Jeanne Marie. II. Carlson, Claudia.
PS595.F32P64 2003
811'.5080375--dc21
                          2002154850

TABLE OF CONTENTS

1. Mapping the Ways

2. Spinning the Tales

3. Voices & Viewpoints

4. Spell Binding & Spell Breaking

5. Magical Objects

6. Desire & Its Discontents

7. The Grimm Sisterhood

8. Variations & Updates

9. Ever After, or a Few Years Later

10. Living the Tales

INTRODUCTION

*It is our intention to present the origin of poetry as a
common possession of the common people which was
not separate from daily life and whose origin mortal eyes
cannot see and which therefore is full of mystery like all
living things.*

The Brothers Grimm, circa 1812

As we write this introduction, a new production of Stephen
Sondheim's *Into the Woods* has opened on Broadway, several new tel-
evision versions of Grimm fairy tales (including *Cinderella*, with
Kathleen Turner well cast as the stepmother) have just been aired,
and an ad for Louis Vuitton that shows the dwarves bearing Snow
White's luggage is running in major magazines. The enchantment
with fairy tales, and a place for fairy tales in people's daily lives, con-
tinues into the 21st century. And the stories collected and written by
the Brothers Grimm, that is by Jacob Grimm (1785–1863) and
Wilhelm Grimm (1786–1859), in seven editions from 1812 to 1857,
remain among the most popular fairy tales in the world today.

It can be difficult to locate the wealth of poetry inspired by fairy
tales among the proliferation of other fairy-tale-related materials. Yet
poetry and fairy tales share common roots of concision and commu-
nal energy derived from an oral tradition. Although the tales can be
expanded into novels, movies, operas, and musicals, many of the orig-
inal stories are no more than a handful of pages in their written ver-
sions. Often sly and intense, these fairy tales, as folklorists remind us,
were not just intended for children, a fact suggested by the original
title of the Brothers Grimm collection: *Kinder- und Hausmärchen*
(*Children's and Household Tales*).

Many 20th century poets grew up reading not only fairy tales but
the 19th century poetry based on them. The Victorian poets were
drawn to legends, myths, and fairy stories, retelling them in often
lengthy formal verse. Alfred Lord Tennyson recreated the ideal of a

passive femininity in "The Sleeping Beauty," (1830; 1842) with the concluding couplet "She sleeps, nor dreams, but ever dwells/ A perfect form in perfect rest," a vision of femininity at odds with the vigor of most female characters in the tales themselves. The pre-Raphaelites embraced fairy tales in paintings and verse. Christina Rossetti's long narrative "Goblin Market" (1862) used familiar fairy-tale elements to tell a tale of sisters tempted by magical food. William Morris's "Rapunzel" (1858) is a verse play in which Rapunzel's name turns out to be Guendolen; Morris infuses the poem with elements of chivalry. This romantic vision and yearning for a golden age didn't challenge or deeply reinvent the tales. And the Victorians chose to largely ignore the more disturbing elements in the original stories.

Though interest in fairy tales never disappears, it does wax and wane, and this is reflected in the poetry of the 20th century. We found substantially more poetry using fairy-tale material from the second half of the century than the first half, owing perhaps to a reaction against all things "Victorian" as the century began as well as the realities of two world wars, economic depression, the rise of social realism, and a fascination with technology and modernism. In the 1960s, a revived enthusiasm for folklore and fantasy was apparent in everything, from clothing styles and music to the popularity of books such as Tolkien's *Lord of the Rings,* and here we begin to see a renewed interest in incorporating fairy-tale elements into poetry.

Around the same time, the women's movement attracted attention to mythic revisionism among many women writers. When Anne Sexton asked her daughter to tell her which of the Grimm tales she liked best, and began writing the poems that would make up her influential collection of fairy-tale poems, *Transformations*, she inspired countless other poets to revisit the tales as a powerful poetic source. This revisioning of fairy tales in contemporary poetry has enabled writers to explore not only their own psyches and crises but many of the most compelling and controversial issues of our time, including sexual politics, class struggles, family dysfunction, child abuse, civil rights, and disease and dying.

The prominence of women in the circulation of fairy tales is a matter of historic record. The Brothers Grimm had many sources for their tales, but "the majority of their informants were women" (Jack Zipes, *The Complete Fairy Tales of the Brothers Grimm*, p 728). They included Dortchen Wild, who married Wilhelm Grimm in 1825. So we were not surprised that we found more poems on this subject authored by women than by men. Have women more likely been the story readers in the family? Is that changing? Do the stories resonate more with women? Certainly, they offer to girls and women prominent stereotypes with which they must grapple—beauty, stepsister, stepmother, witch, crone, princess, and of course "prince charming." By devoting a chapter to this Grimm Sisterhood, we mean only to nod to the legacy of women's involvement with fairy-tale transmission. We hope the complications of such a category, as discussed in the poems, will speak for themselves.

◆　◆　◆

When we began to gather poems for this anthology, we had thought we would include any poem found on the topic, but we quickly realized the impracticality of that approach. For one thing there were many more than we had anticipated. In addition, some poems were too similar, some too long, while others simply could not be worked into the structure of the book as it began to take shape. Once we tracked down Wolfgang Mieder's out-of-print 1985 anthology of fairy-tale poetry, *Disenchantments*, we realized we did not want to repeat all his selections, yet a few seemed too essential to leave out if our anthology was to be as comprehensive as we had planned. As it turns out, we have included 14 of the 78 authors Mieder included, but not all are represented by the same poems. This collection is weighted more heavily toward the last half of the 20th century, including a generous sampling of the substantial body of fairy-tale poetry that has been published since 1985. We hope this anthology complements Mieder's book while also expanding upon it, and we acknowledge our debt to his work in this field.

In the interest of providing historical context and range, we have included a poem of Amy Lowell's from her 1912 debut collection, the oldest poem in this anthology, and a few poems written in the first year or so of the 21st century. Some of the poems selected are well known, such as the poem from Sexton's *Transformations* and also those from Sara Henderson Hay's *Story Hour*. But because these books are still in print and widely available, we have reprinted only a few poems from such better known sources to leave room for the work drawn from diverse books and journals, many of which are out of print or hard to find. In addition, some of these poems are appearing in print for the first time. To keep this anthology a reasonable size, we decided to include only poems written in English, although the Grimm tales are known worldwide, and many fine translations of fairy-tale poems exist from world literature. And here let us note that in the case of poems from the United Kingdom and Australia, we have retained British spellings while standardizing some punctuation.

While in principle we limited our selection to poems based on tales of the Brothers Grimm, we readily admit that we could not always be purists about this criterion. Poets are usually working from their memories of the tales, and these are often a mixture of elements from various versions, films, cartoons, and other popularizations—sometimes not strictly Grimm elements. One notable example is the image of "kissing the frog." In the Grimm tale, "The Frog King," the frog is not kissed but rather thrown against the wall by an exasperated princess. Nevertheless, the frog-kissing action has been added to the story so often that it has become, to most people, an essential ingredient. We regard such permutations as interesting aspects of the way tales get handed down and passed on. But we would encourage all readers to return to the actual Grimm source for what is often an eye-opening "refresher course." Likewise, savvy readers will detect details from the French versions of tales or a bit of Hans Christian Andersen here and there, but all the poems include some elements that are specifically Grimm and most are predominantly so (therefore poems that address exclusively non-Grimm tales such as "Goldilocks" or "Beauty and the Beast" are not included).

Alongside memory, there is of course the poet's imagination that sets to work in these poems, and that too contributes to the tale-bending, tale-embellishing, "misremembering," updating, and idiosyncratic transforming of the tales. Poets often reshape the stories to meet psychological or autobiographical needs and circumstances. The elasticity of the tales in the hands of these poets was something that constantly fascinated and delighted us. It was one of the chief aspects that attracted us to this project from the start and one we trust readers will appreciate and enjoy. In addition, the variety of poetic techniques and approaches displayed here, selected without prejudice toward certain formal or free styles, is a facet of 20th century poetry that we wanted to represent. A rich formal virtuosity, from the abecedarian poem to the sonnet, including a number of inventive nonce forms, is to be found. And a range of tone, from the instructive to the elegaic, from the hilarious to the horrific, was another aspect of this poetry we wanted to showcase. One trend in the 20th century fairy-tale poem worth noting is the dominance of the dramatic monologue or "persona poem" to explore the characters and situations of the tales and give them contemporary twists. We have one chapter that explores this exclusively (Voices & Viewpoints), but these poems can be found throughout the collection.

With regard to the chapters of this anthology, they are intended to provide a thematic but not inflexible organization. Many poems could have been quite happily and appropriately placed in two or three chapters. We strove for a trail of dynamic juxtapositions and associations that would move about the tales with some abandon. While it is interesting at times to group poems about a single tale together—and the reader will find a number of these "miniseries" throughout—too many in a row begins to feel repetitive and denies the subtler attributes that link some of these poems. We suspect that few anthologies get read sequentially from start to finish, but should a reader be so inclined, we tried to make that route a rewarding and revealing one. For those wanting to make a study of poems about one specific tale, we have provided an Index of Poems by Tale (p 283) to show the way. While a balance of "intratale" and "intertale" considerations guided our ordering, we hope that readers will make their own leaps and find their own paths and connections.

These poems reveal the complex relationship that exists between contemporary poets and a received body of myth or lore. The Grimm tales are subject to a significant amount of skepticism, of refutation or "talking back," and of fracturing or breaking down. Yet an abiding, if irreverent, affection and appreciation for the tales, an acknowledgment of their continuing pull and metaphoric power also can be discerned. There is a mutual enrichment when poets become tale (re)tellers: the poets keep the stories current and fresh and give them back their original vivacity, rigor, and immediacy, while the stories enable the poets to tap into a vast and resonant source of symbol and cultural history. The tales become again "full of mystery like all living things," released from the confines of the nursery, rescued from ossification or sentimentalization, able again to fill us with wonder, dread, and delight.

◆ ◆ ◆

In closing, we want to express our appreciation to all who sent us work to consider. They have convinced us that the mining of fairy tales for the making of poems proceeds unabated in the new century. We are grateful to the many friends who have encouraged us in this project along the way, and we wish to send special thanks to a few whose help was invaluable: to Kathleen Crown, David Cappella, and the late Marcia Lipson, for their voices and letters of support; to Aldo Alvarez, David Trinidad, and Terri Windling for their enthusiasm and guidance toward many fine poets and poems; to the staff at Poets House where much of our research was done; to Ruth B. Bottigheimer, Dana Gioia, and Annie Finch for their generous advice; to Heidi Anne Heiner for helping with the cover; to Fred Courtright for guiding us through the permissions brambles; to Bob Mendelsohn and Jim Racheff who always appeared with sustaining words and refreshments at just the right moment; and to Robert McDowell, for sharing the vision.

Jeanne Marie Beaumont
& Claudia Carlson
New York City
Fall 2002

MAPPING THE WAYS

serious as lines on a map or instructions in a secret book...

SANDRA M. GILBERT

walk toward what
you don't know

KATHLEEN JESME

you never wanted, did you, a journey as simple as that?

ELIZABETH SPIRES

SANDRA M. GILBERT

Landscape: In the Forest

Midnight. The witch's hut
splits like a pomegranate.
Dried flowers pour from seams in the wall.
The floorboards shiver, shred, caress
themselves with splintery claws,
pine needles, in love with their own scent.

And now the forest, where only this evening
the coaches of princes clattered,
is silent—the ladies vanished like light,
the fur, the velvet—and now
the witch in her child clothing
wanders among green branches,

her skin the wax of berries, her feathery hair
innocent as new leaves.

LISEL MUELLER

Voices from the Forest

1 THE VOICE OF THE TRAVELER WHO ESCAPED

No matter how exhausted you are,
and though you think you will die of thirst,
do not enter the house in the forest.
Ignore the unlocked door
and the lamp in the window, lit for you.
Pass the house, which is real
and warm and apparently safe,
where the traveler is received
by someone, or at least
by a fire and a spread table.
It is only when you finish eating
and, drowsy and grateful, pull off your shoes,
that the ax falls or the giant returns
or the monster springs or the witch
locks the door from the outside
and throws away the key.

2 WARNING TO VIRGINS

Each year you become more wary,
less easily taken in,
but my disguises still fool you.
Today I will go as the bear
who lumbers to the door
of two young beauties, to be brushed
and petted, and to eat
out of their hands. Yesterday
I was the prince of frogs
hopping up golden stairs
to sheets that smelled of the sun.
Tomorrow I'll live, an unspecified beast,
in a marvelous castle, enjoying
the echo chamber, my godlike roar.
You know the girl, and how
she will discover the human.
But I'm not through: I'll come

and trick you, long-legged darling,
baby blond, with my wizened face,
my dwarf's cap and ridiculous voice.
Watch out for little men
at crossroads, who give you directions
and ask to share your supper:
one slip of the tongue, and you lose.
There is no second chance.

3 A VOICE FROM OUT OF THE NIGHT

Remember me, I was a celebrity,
the famous beauty. All mirrors confirmed me,
the panel of judges ogled me
and cast a unanimous vote.
I was asked my opinion
on marriage, men, abortion,
the use of liquor and drugs;
that was a long time ago.

When my voice deepened
and a bristle
appeared under my chin,
when my blond hair
developed gray roots
and my waist thickened,
the rumors started.
When my legs became sticks
and small brown toads
spotted the backs of my hands,
everyone believed them.
I was accused of devouring children
and mutilating men;
they said I smelled of old age
and strong home remedies.
They cast me into the forest
but come to me secretly, in the dark,
in their times of trouble.
What could I have done to convince them
I was not guilty?
Loss of beauty was all
the proof they needed.

Young wives in love with your men,
kissing your babies: this
could be a warning, but what is the use?
Husbands will flee you,
sons will turn on you,
daughters will throw up their hands
and cry, "Not me! Not me!"

4 THE HUNTER'S VOICE

Happily, I am exempt
from your bazaar of punishments
and rewards, the way you pass out beauty
and hold the burning shoes in abeyance
until the pendulum swings.
I will accept an assignment
from anyone who pays me,
and if the heart I bring back as proof
is not the intended one,
who is to know? I wear green,
not your colors of blood and snow;
I disappear among trees
and am not missed.
You would never believe
I have changed the plot of your lives.

5 THE FALSE BRIDE'S SIDE OF THE STORY

Kindness ran in your blood,
poverty spiked mine.

Nature gave you beauty,
mine came from tubes of paint.

You were a trusting fool,
I tried to take care of myself.

You wept genuine diamonds,
I wept plain salt tears.

You kept warm in a paper dress,
I froze in furs and woolens.

You found love without trying,
I took your lover but failed at love.

Your wedding ring kept shining,
mine turned black the first night.

Your baby was plump and bright-eyed,
mine was a monster disguised as a child.

Sister, my soul, my twin
on the other end of our seesaw,
any moment now
you will rise to the top, resurrected,
your cheeks swelling like plums,
while I go down to my death.
There the story breaks off
for the sake of the children who listen,
but don't be too sure. One day,
one afternoon, as you sit
(a calm Vermeer in sunlight)
counting your blessings like stitches,
I may step out of the sun,
large and dark as life.

6 THE THIRD SON'S CONFESSION

Early on I was chosen
the one least likely to succeed.
I was made fun of, but got away
with daydreaming and learning the language
of wood doves and white snakes.
My brothers were ambitious
and steady; they made maps
of possible trails through the forest,
they trained for months
for the climb up the glass mountain,
they monitored their shudders
to overcome fear on the field of bones.
I wished them luck, but they failed,
they came home defeated and bitter,
and I, late bloomer intending nothing,
found myself on the other side

of the forest, across the boneyard,
on top of the glass mountain.
Don't ask me if I was chosen
or simply lucky. Years ago
I threw a penny down a well,
but I've forgotten the wish.

7 FLESH AND BLOOD

This is my brother the fat, caged boy
This is my brother the spotted fawn
These are my brothers the seven ravens
These are my brothers the six mute swans

I have a plan for my brother the boy
I have a hermit's shack for my fawn
I've cut off a finger to save my ravens
I've given up speech to save my swans

"Help me," whispers my brother the boy
"Play with me," begs my high-stepping fawn
"Why were you born," lament the ravens
"You caused our exile," accuse the swans

Brothers, my brothers, I am your sister
I am a woman, I will be a wife
I am your face in the altered mirror
I will give you back your life

Brother my boy, you'll grow thin and forget me
You'll play with another, brother my fawn
Human, my seven, you will hunt ravens
Human, you'll leave me, my six mute swans

8 THE VOICE FROM UNDER THE HAZEL BUSH

I died for you. Each spring
I wake in my house of roots;
my memory leafs out
into a rich green dress
for you to dance in. The moon
turns it to silver, the evening sun

to gold. Be happy, my daughter.
You think I have magic powers,
others call it love.
I tell you it is the will
to survive, in you, in the earth.
Your story does not end
with the wedding dance, it goes on.

KATHLEEN JESME

Afraid to Look Afraid to Look Away

Moonlight breaks on the fir trees
in the deep forest
she waits for you.

The garden of stones casts
shadows
hover on the ground.

The breadcrumbs are
the old trail
of pebbles is white in

the moonlight
has no beginning.

Leave this false trail
and all trails:

walk toward what
you don't know
the moon will take you there.

The house is
gingerbread and sugar
will fill you up at first.

You will think you
have found childhood.

But she is inside
what you eat
devours you.

Stay with her, let her feed you
as she will
stoke her oven.

Keep your brother safe from
her dim eyes
cannot see you.

Wait for her to go to
the fire
will move you.

You must stay and
watch her burn if you forget
and look away

you will forget.

Now the fire burns on
in the garden
you wake the stones.

ANDREA HOLLANDER BUDY

Asleep in the Forest

after Hansel & Grettel,
a painting by Monique Felix

They might have been lovers,
but lovers do not sleep

as close as this: stretched out
in the forest's sanctuary

as if God were about
instead of a witch.

Or else they sleep closer, hoping
closeness will be a kind of latch,

a madcap brace against the loneliness
they sense in happy endings.

They bend the story now and then,
remember the fox, the frog, the beauty

always hiding somewhere deeper than they've been.
Their sleep is innocent and blue

and they keep counting on togetherness
to take them in and bring them safely out.

They'd follow stars,
but stars don't penetrate this forest.

They follow lightning
bugs instead, as if the light itself

were all that mattered.
It's this mistake

that took them to the witch's house,
the first of many.

But not tonight.
Tonight they take their sleep

as we might step into a creek
together, and linger in it, let

what is bad
rise to the surface, unnoticed

for a moment, clouding the water,
then rinse itself away,

as we look only into
one another's eyes at what is good,

and know that that is all there is
and it will stay.

MARY JO BANG

Gretel

Mother, I am bare in a mist-mad forest.
Only the moon shows me love.

Winter will crush me: tiny arms, pale feet,
tongue of rust. I have a thousand visions:

you ironing an enormous dress; eating
chocolate and honey, sausage

and a luscious peach; the sun drunk
and easy; spring blowing raw sky

and storm scream; someone running.
You cry, *Go, go. Take them, will you?*

He does, along the sea road with its
stopped ship fast asleep. In this place

of elaborate beauty, it is late autumn
and mostly quiet, except when

the heaven-born wind wags and flaps
the branch he left tied

to a sere white ash. Silence itself is strategy,
a signed language,

gorgeous, fluid in the hands
of those who learned it in childhood.

You know we were never meant
to live here, only to learn *relinquished*,

forsworn, to grasp with wet hands the cold
metal of life, then find a way to let go.

ELIZABETH SPIRES

Black Fairy Tale

Who were you that day you left your parents
standing on the platform, waving black handkerchiefs
—How young they were then!—
and you waving back, you with money in your pocket
      and your grin,
as the train began to move, first slowly, then slowly
speeding up, the whitewashed houses of that village
falling flatly back into the past
as you sped forward into a morning stilled by fog,
by enchantment, dreaming of a woman
bending over you, pouring milk into a glass,
whispering, *Drink this, Drink this.*

So many years have passed!
You wake to the noon sun burning a hard, black outline
around the fallow fields, the shimmering trees and houses,
shadows doubled into themselves, hiding,
the train speeding faster, ever faster,
birds on the wires, black birds,
marking off milestones, chuckling to themselves.
Smiles, gestures, currency, the few words
your parents taught you, like *love, farewell,* and *courage,*
are useless now, you're crossing unfamiliar borders
quickly, much too quickly, your death and birth connected,
as the crow flies, by a straight line on a map
although you never wanted, did you, a journey as simple as that?

For one ten thousandth of a second
you stall at midpoint, caught between twin cities,
twin infinities, just long enough to glimpse
a pale child beckoning from the black edge of the forest.
Return, you must return, by following the black fairy tale,
the one your parents kept from you,
locked in the black book at the back of the closet.
Bits of bread, fluttering rags snagged on hedges,
will show you the way if you look, if you look.

Who must you save? Shadows are showing themselves,
touching this thing and that with their shadowy spells,
a fat red sun is disappearing as you enter
the clearing where the empty cottage stands,
its door swinging on hinges that sing, *What use, What use.*
Nobody's there, nobody that is
except a crow, hunched in a tree,
its feathers coal-black and shining, eyeballing you,
each eye as empty as the barrel of a gun,
making a *click, click, click,*
now that you've arrived.

ELAINE EQUI

Further Adventures

The bird carries her off in its beak
her prettiness
    (ribbon   heart's rouge)
straining against flight, doing what she never
dreamed (actually, what she often dreamed
but never dared).   Up high
one can see the breath of Time,
its cold exhale. Time has carried her off
and the world is rearing up on hind legs
like the statue of a general on his horse.
The girl carries the world off
    (its prettiness and twin ugliness)
as surely as she is carried, yet can't stop
feeling she has forgotten something:
a necklace of beads, a train of thought,
a funeral procession with a broken clasp.
Something shining *beneath* the world
    (a word   a charm).
Something is calling her back.

SANDRA M. GILBERT

The Twelve Dancing Princesses

1

Why am I distracted all day, dreaming of the twelve princesses,
their heavy satin skirts, their swift flight across dark fields, their slow
cold sensual descent into the lake? All day the twelve princesses
circle my furniture like gulls, crying out in a strange language,
proposing mysterious patterns with their wings. Below them
indecipherable ripples wash over the carpet like white lies.

At midnight the gates of the lake swing wide: the princesses enter
the halls of water. In that blue-green ballroom they dance like
minnows, darting among stones, leaping away from circles of light.
Even as I write these words, each solitary dancer is spinning in the
palace of shadow, spinning through night so deep that the call of
the owl is not heard, and the twelve underground princes, wrapped
in sleep, row silently away across the lake.

2

I am the scholar of the dark armchair—the crimson wingchair of
1945, the overstuffed gold-tufted armchair of 1948, the downy satin
chair of 1952, and always the dark chair beneath, the chair immense
as the lap of a grandfather, the chair in which I sit reading the tale
of the twelve dancing princesses.

Winter. Wind on the fire escape. The hush of snow. Summer.
Shouts in the street. Horns, bells, processions of cars. I curl myself
into the dark armchair. I shape my body to its shape, I do not lift
my eyes.

Miles away, at the edge of the city, the twelve princesses flee
toward the airfield. Night swells the arms of the chair that holds me.
The princesses dance in the sky like helicopters. Below them the
lights of the runway burn in silence, serious as lines on a map or
instructions in a secret book: severe frontiers, all crossing forbidden.

DONALD FINKEL

The Sleeping Kingdom

from The Hero

The horses stand up again and shake themselves,
the flies stir on the wall, the fire brightens,
the maid goes on plucking the chicken, and the cook
gives such a slap to the scullery boy he yells.

For three years now it has been like that every morning;
and watching the horses wheel, the dogs in snow,
the thrill is not diminished. The wise were wrong:
you can never have too much of a good thing.

No, with a little luck, and moderate taxes,
it should keep going. Even in off years
the wine is passable; and who can kick
if the crops are plentiful and the people happy?

For a while I walked the corridors when I came.
In every room they hung like tapestries,
as if time had snagged on the nail of four o'clock,
at day's dead center, banal afternoon:

the throne-room empty but for one maid,
dusting and dusting a mantel; upstairs a guest
climbed forever into his dinner clothes;
neither the night begun nor the day ended.

And yet the dailiest gesture seemed to me,
simply by virtue of its hanging there,
translucent and inevitable and fine.
Even the dust stayed dancing in the sun

in formal patterns. I thought, And who am I
to blow like a wind behind such attitudes?
Having no use for perfection, however, they thank me.
Later in the tower, watching those little breasts

lift toward me imperceptibly, and fall,
I felt desire sprout in the dark like a tuber.
But bending my mouth to that perfect mouth I wondered
from what it was I had meant to save this kingdom.

DEBORA GREGER

Briar Rose

Where is paradise without the gate?
Ask any gardener, his bags of bone meal busy
    keeping the weedy world at bay.

Within its boxwood walls, like that great kitchen
    the cook hungered after,
a place for everything, and everything in it

    named by scholar and scullery maid:
between *Rosa canina* and *foetida,* next to "Adam"
    and "Little White Pet," the briar

a mother's thorned thanksgiving named me for,
    pricking the very air's approach.
Ask any man with sense enough not to try for me

    that century I slept in state:
men who did wound up as bones of stories
    tendril by barbed tendril woven,

sentence by overgrown sentence, into mine—
    all but you, the thicket parting,
thorns going soft as you breezed past.

    What is paradise without a gate?
I slept the sleep of that first man who slept so deep
    he didn't miss the bone he gave up.

What must his waking words have been? *Is it you?*
    How long you have kept me waiting.
I give him mine. Given back a voice gone feral,

    that squeaked and croaked,
I gave you a talking-to cut off by your long—
    no, the briefest kiss.

Think of your gardens when we're not there.
  No longer does the moorhen cross the pond
on stepping stones of lily pads that if it rushes

  bear its feathered weight.

NEIL GAIMAN

Instructions

Touch the wooden gate in the wall you never
    saw before.
Say "please" before you open the latch,
go through,
walk down the path.
A red metal imp hangs from the green-painted
    front door,
as a knocker,
do not touch it; it will bite your fingers.
Walk through the house. Take nothing. Eat
    nothing.
However,
if any creature tells you that it hungers,
feed it.
If it tells you that it is dirty,
clean it.
If it cries to you that it hurts,
if you can,
ease its pain.

From the back garden you will be able to see the
    wild wood.
The deep well you walk past leads to Winter's
    realm;
there is another land at the bottom of it.
If you turn around here,
you can walk back, safely;
you will lose no face. I will think no less of you.

Once through the garden you will be in the
    wood.
The trees are old. Eyes peer from the under-
    growth.
Beneath a twisted oak sits an old woman. She
    may ask for something;
give it to her. She
will point the way to the castle.
Inside it are three princesses.

Do not trust the youngest. Walk on.
In the clearing beyond the castle the twelve
    months sit about a fire,
warming their feet, exchanging tales.
They may do favors for you, if you are polite.
You may pick strawberries in December's frost.

Trust the wolves, but do not tell them where
    you are going.
The river can be crossed by the ferry. The ferry-
    man will take you.
(The answer to his question is this:
If he hands the oar to his passenger, he will be free to
    leave the boat.
Only tell him this from a safe distance.)

If an eagle gives you a feather, keep it safe.
Remember: that giants sleep too soundly; that
witches are often betrayed by their appetites;
dragons have one soft spot, somewhere, always;
hearts can be well-hidden,
and you betray them with your tongue.

Do not be jealous of your sister.
Know that diamonds and roses
are as uncomfortable when they tumble from
    one's lips as toads and frogs:
colder, too, and sharper, and they cut.

Remember your name.
Do not lose hope—what you seek will be found.
Trust ghosts. Trust those that you have helped
    to help you in their turn.
Trust dreams.
Trust your heart, and trust your story.

When you come back, return the way you came.
Favors will be returned, debts be repaid.
Do not forget your manners.
Do not look back.
Ride the wise eagle (you shall not fall).
Ride the silver fish (you will not drown).
Ride the gray wolf (hold tightly to his fur).

There is a worm at the heart of the tower; that is
    why it will not stand.

When you reach the little house, the place your
    journey started,
you will recognize it, although it will seem
    much smaller than you remember.
Walk up the path, and through the garden gate
    you never saw before but once.
And then go home. Or make a home.

Or rest.

JEANNE MARIE BEAUMONT

Hotel Grimm

There was once a maid . . .

Its address was on the creased napkin
that escaped your hand and danced away
in the wind. You only find the place
because it's changed beyond recognition.
The doorman's ugly in wolf's clothing—not
your type at all—brown eyes begging for business
like a lounge lit all the long rainy day.
There's a new bar where the frogs hang.
"I preferred it as The Palace," one croaks.
You say, "And you were the prince?"
"Touché." Only your glasses touch.
The mirrors are gossips; they tell you
what you don't look like. Flies doze on the walls.
Wish for wings here and you'll be given arms.
The tower's occupied. Your room is a forest.
"In the hollow of a tree you will sleep till morning."
"But your sign says *Giant-size beds*," you protest.
"Wish for more wishes, you'll be sent to wash dishes."
You eavesdrop at dinner on the old man and woman:
". . . just as I was closing my eyes
the bed began to move about the room."
"That's nothing. I lay down by the fire
and woke in the mouth of a cow."
No one's complaining. They get what
they've come for: three-night minimum,
a box of gingerbread to bring back to their kin.
You may lie awake all night pondering
your next wish. Then a long apprenticeship begins
—if you wish for wisdom, as you should. Stay a spell.
Call up maid service for the faun's back pillow.
Step lightly over those snorers in the hall.
You cannot sleep too much, your hair cannot
be too long, your foot cannot be
too small.

AMY GERSTLER

Lost in the Forest

I'd given up hope. Hadn't eaten in three
days. Resigned to being wolf meat . . .
when, unbelievably, I found myself in
a clearing. Two goats with bells
round their necks stared at me:
their pupils like coin slots
in piggy banks. I could have gotten
the truth out of those two,
if goats spoke. I saw leeks
and radishes planted in rows;
wash billowing on a clothesline . . .
and the innocuous-looking cottage
in the woods with its lapping tongue
of a welcome mat slurped me in.

In the kitchen, a woman so old her sex
is barely discernible pours a glass
of fraudulent milk. I'm so hungry
my hand shakes. But what is this liquid?
"Drink up, sweetheart," she says,
and as I wipe the white mustache
off with the back of my hand:
"Atta girl." Have I stumbled
into the clutches of St. Somebody?
Who can tell. "You'll find I prevail here
in my own little kingdom," she says as
she leads me upstairs—her bony grip
on my arm a proclamation of ownership,
as though I've always been hers.

HENRY SLOSS

Fairy Tales

Seeing the courted, won, become
So like the frog one kissed,
A lesson seems to beckon *psst* . . .

The wretchedness of rag and besom,
Though sisters run it down,
Hurts less than watching Prince turn clown.

Dispell the charmer in your bosom
Before he reappears
Beside you, smiling through your tears.

Take a beldam's advice and buy some
Property on a beach
Desire's bedlam cannot reach.

Give up the yearning to be some
One other than you are;
Surgery leaves a scar.

She took my hand then, moved by some
Impulse or another,
And croaked, *Come, darling, kiss godmother*.

2

SPINNING
THE TALES

Couldn't there be, for me,
just one more fairytale?
MONA VAN DUYN

Hate transforms the same as love
JOYCE THOMAS

ELLEN BRYANT VOIGT

Fairy Tale

The wronged spirit brought the child
a basket of riches:
two parents, justice and mercy;
a beauty both stunning and organic;
fame beyond the wide walls of the castle;
and intelligence, lying like an asp
at the bottom of the basket.
With this last gift she could discern
the flaw in nature
and all of nature's fruits.

Thus she came to her
majority already skilled,
having pressed bright flowers
to a film, having memorized
the verses of the day.
For months, she did not eat,
she did not traffic with the agencies
of change: she had cast her will entirely

against decay. Even when
the wild tangle emerged
from the careful lawns, and ebony birds
came down from the woods
to roost in the chiseled turrets
and foul the court, she would not stir
nor in any way disturb
the triumph that would greet the shallow prince:
a soul unencumbered
in a neutral body.

ANNE SEXTON

The Twelve Dancing Princesses

If you danced from midnight
to six A.M. who would understand?

The runaway boy
who chucks it all
to live on the Boston Common
on speed and saltines,
pissing in the duck pond,
rapping with the street priest,
trading talk like blows,
another missing person,
would understand.

The paralytic's wife
who takes her love to town,
sitting on the bar stool,
downing stingers and peanuts,
singing "That ole Ace down in the hole,"
would understand.

The passengers
from Boston to Paris
watching the movie with dawn
coming up like statues of honey,
having partaken of champagne and steak
while the world turned like a toy globe,
those murderers of the nightgown
would understand.

The amnesiac
who tunes into a new neighborhood,
having misplaced the past,
having thrown out someone else's
credit cards and monogrammed watch,
would understand.

The drunken poet
(a genius by daylight)
who places long-distance calls

at three A.M. and then lets you sit
holding the phone while he vomits
(he calls it "The Night of the Long Knives")
getting his kicks out of the death call,
would understand.

The insomniac
listening to his heart
thumping like a June bug,
listening on his transistor
to Long John Nebel arguing from New York,
lying on his bed like a stone table,
would understand.

The night nurse
with her eyes slit like Venetian blinds,
she of the tubes and the plasma,
listening to the heart monitor,
the death cricket bleeping,
she who calls you "we"
and keeps vigil like a ballistic missile,
would understand.

Once
this king had twelve daughters,
each more beautiful than the other.
They slept together, bed by bed
in a kind of girls' dormitory.
At night the king locked and bolted the door.
How could they possibly escape?
Yet each morning their shoes
were danced to pieces.
Each was as worn as an old jockstrap.
The king sent out a proclamation
that anyone who could discover
where the princesses did their dancing
could take his pick of the litter.
However there was a catch.
If he failed, he would pay with his life.
Well, so it goes.

Many princes tried,
each sitting outside the dormitory,
the door ajar so he could observe

what enchantment came over the shoes.
But each time the twelve dancing princesses
gave the snoopy man a Mickey Finn
and so he was beheaded.
Poof! Like a basketball.

It so happened that a poor soldier
heard about these strange goings on
and decided to give it a try.
On his way to the castle
he met an old woman.
Age, for a change, was of some use.
She wasn't stuffed in a nursing home.
She told him not to drink a drop of wine
and gave him a cloak that would make
him invisible when the right time came.
And thus he sat outside the dorm.
The oldest princess brought him some wine
but he fastened a sponge beneath his chin,
looking the opposite of Andy Gump.

The sponge soaked up the wine,
and thus he stayed awake.
He feigned sleep however
and the princesses sprang out of their beds
and fussed around like a Miss America Contest.
Then the eldest went to her bed
and knocked upon it and it sank into the earth.
They descended down the opening
one after the other. The crafty soldier
put on his invisible cloak and followed.
Yikes, said the youngest daughter,
something just stepped on my dress.
But the oldest thought it just a nail.

Next stood an avenue of trees,
each leaf made of sterling silver.
The soldier took a leaf for proof.
The youngest heard the branch break
and said, Oof! Who goes there?
But the oldest said, Those are
the royal trumpets playing triumphantly.
The next trees were made of diamonds.

He took one that flickered like Tinkerbell
and the youngest said: Wait up! He is here!
But the oldest said: Trumpets, my dear.

Next they came to a lake where lay
twelve boats with twelve enchanted princes
waiting to row them to the underground castle.
The soldier sat in the youngest's boat
and the boat was as heavy as if an icebox
had been added but the prince did not suspect.

Next came the ball where the shoes did duty.
The princesses danced like taxi girls at Roseland
as if those tickets would run right out.
They were painted in kisses with their secret hair
and though the soldier drank from their cups
they drank down their youth with nary a thought.
Cruets of champagne and cups full of rubies.
They danced until morning and the sun came up
naked and angry and so they returned
by the same strange route. The soldier
went forward through the dormitory and into
his waiting chair to feign his druggy sleep.
That morning the soldier, his eyes fiery
like blood in a wound, his purpose brutal
as if facing a battle, hurried with his answer
as if to the Sphinx. The shoes! The shoes!
The soldier told. He brought forth
the silver leaf, the diamond the size of a plum.

He had won. The dancing shoes would dance
no more. The princesses were torn from
their night life like a baby from its pacifier.
Because he was old he picked the eldest.
At the wedding the princesses averted their eyes
and sagged like old sweatshirts.
Now the runaways would run no more and never
again would their hair be tangled into diamonds,
never again their shoes worn down to a laugh,
never the bed falling down into purgatory
to let them climb in after
with their Lucifer kicking.

MARTHA CARLSON-BRADLEY

The Maiden Without Hands

And the father takes
his daughter's hand
firmly in his own,

reeking as he wields the ax
of cows, sweat,
the knuckles that trap her
cracked and red.

She will not turn her eyes away,

demands that her severed arms
be strapped to her back,
young woman on a country road

who walks towards strangers.

MARTHA CARLSON-BRADLEY

The White Snake

One taste of the white snake
prepared like a feast on a tray

and the young man's landscape
scintillates with voices—prate
of sparrows, rage of ants.

Caught in the reeds
fish plead for rescue,

the horse he slays
to feed the fledgling ravens
mute in its own defense.

JANET MCADAMS

The Sister of the Swans

The sister roamed the world to find them:
her six brothers, changed by a father's
thoughtless wish. In the forest cottage
where she found them, they ate from swan-
sized plates and slept in beds too cramped
for their human sister. For years,
they lived like this: between two worlds.
The sister slept on a pallet when she found them.

The sister rode on a net across the ocean,
like a web carried in the beaks of six
spiders. She took the spell's vow of silence
before she met the King, who loved her
for her modest ways. He was sure she nodded
the day his huntsmen dragged her
to the castle and he asked her to marry.
Six of the seven years he loved her less and less.

For seven years she worked at night to sew
the six nettle shirts that would release
her brothers. She gathered the stinging
nettles from the neglected graves of children.
The King shared no part of this story.
Her modest glances turned to secretive looks
and the Queen Mother whispered: *See how she
steals from your bed late at night.*

Late at night, the King imagined one young
lover then another. Still, she could not speak.
She moved easily through the air, like her mute swan
brothers, as she gathered the nettles in silence.
The swan brothers saved her from the King's harsh
punishment in the nick of time. Their wings beat out
the flames, their beaks pulled loose the cords that bound her,
as the grieving King looked on in love and hatred.

Of course, the grieving King rejoiced to see
the long spell broken, when the brothers put on
the shirts that transformed them. But there were
so many brothers. The youngest was saved
by a shirt with one sleeve missing. Sickened, the King
averted his glance. His wife's voice was low and rough,
not at all the way he'd imagined. He wondered
at the lullaby she sang the prince, a boy with downy hair.

The swan princes' wild laughter rang out in the castle.
The Queen put her loom away: she was tired of weaving.
Once, the King heard her hiss at the cook. At night,
hands burning with the memory of nettles, the King snoring
uneasily beside her, did she long for the midnight churchyard?
The King longed for the sweet girl he married,
each time he heard the graceful swish of her garments
or felt her elegant white neck between his hands.

DENISE LEVERTOV

An Embroidery (I)

Rose Red's hair is brown as fur
and shines in firelight as she prepares
supper of honey and apples, curds and whey,
for the bear, and leaves it ready
on the hearth-stone.

Rose White's gray eyes
look into the dark forest.

Rose Red's cheeks are burning,
sign of her ardent, joyful
compassionate heart.
Rose White is pale,
turning away when she hears
the bear's paw on the latch.

When he enters, there is
frost on his fur,
he draws near to the fire
giving off sparks.
Rose White catches the scent of the forest,
of mushrooms, of rosin.

Together Rose Red and Rose White
sing to the bear;
it is a cradle song, a loom song,
a song about marriage, about
a pilgrimage to the mountains
long ago.
        Raised on an elbow,
the bear stretched on the hearth
nods and hums; soon he sighs
and puts down his head.

He sleeps; the Roses
bank the fire.
Sunk in the clouds of their feather bed
they prepare to dream.

Rose Red in a cave that smells of honey
dreams she is combing the fur of her cubs
with a golden comb.
Rose White is lying awake.

Rose White shall marry the bear's brother.
Shall he too
when the time is ripe,
step from the bear's hide?
Is that other, her bridegroom,
here in the room?

MONA VAN DUYN

Cinderella's Story

To tell you the truth, the shoe pinched.
I had no way of knowing, you see,
that I was the girl he'd dreamed of.
Imagination had always consoled me,
but I'd tried to use it with care.
My sisters, I'd always thought, were the family
romantics, expecting nice clothes to do the trick
instead of the beholder's transforming eye.
All that dancing I would have to have done,
if it *was* me, had made my feet swollen.
But I didn't know I'd been dancing, I thought him a dreamer.
He had everything—looks, loneliness,
the belief that comforting and love could cure
even an advanced neurosis.
I didn't know whether or not
he was deluded, but I was sure
he was brave. I wanted to have worn the slipper.

And that's all there was to the first transformation,
something that happened so fast I nearly lost it
with one disclaiming murmur, but something
that did happen, that he made me believe.

None of my skills but love was the slightest use
to my husband. Others did well at keeping
the home fires damped or hot.
And so I began to learn the sleeping
senses. I learned wholly to love
the man in the prince, what didn't dance:
bad breath in the morning, sexual clumsiness,
a childlike willingness to let the old queen
dominate. That was easy. And I read a lot.
Snarled in ideas, heading for the unseen,
I heard the wise men snicker when I spoke.
I learned that I had some beauty and, wearing
one gown or another for my husband's sake,
I learned of its very real enhancement.

That was a little harder. I had a ball
before I learned to use what beauty I had
with kindness and honor. That was hardest of all.
Our son was born, and I went to the child
through a clutter of nursemaids to tell him
how it feels to be poor. I started to grow old.
My husband saw everything and was grateful.
Thickening a bit at the waist, he firmed
and stayed, always, faithful.

And that was the second transformation,
slow and solid.
We were happy together.

Everything comes in three's, they say,
and I'm stuck in the third transformation,
flopping like a fish who's out of the life-saving
everyday water. I starve now for a ration
of dreams, I've never learned to live
without dreams. All through the filth and anger
of childhood I ate them like a calming sugar,
my sweet secret. I move through the palace,
gripping its ghostly furniture
till my fingers ache. I guess
that it is real, that I am living,
but what is there left to dream of?
I dream, day and night, of giving.

Prince, soon to be king,
we've made all our lovely exchanges
and my years as your princess are ending.
Couldn't there be, for me,
just one more fairytale?
More fiercely than the silliest clubwoman
in the kingdom, I try to hold onto my looks
because I dream that there was someone
warted, once upon a time,
waiting a kiss to tell him he too
could be beloved. My frog,
my frog, where shall I find you?

JOYCE THOMAS

The Frog Prince

His is the best fairy tale.

It has something for everyone in it—
    a king, a princess
    an absent mother, the frog
    a tease of sex, splattering
    of violence, even
    a golden ball.

Three iridescent bubbles,
the frog's wishes rise (let me
    eat from your plate, let me
    drink from your cup, let me
    sleep in your bed) up the ladder of courtship
    while serving as a legal contract
    the princess seals with her lips,
    not thinking daddy will hold her to it.
Clearly she is naïve,
stands in the wetlands of adolescence.

The frog's desire is plain as
his aching smile:
    he would be human at any price
    and barters the marsh for crockery
    and pewter, the square corners
    of her fitted sheets.
His is the passion for change.

Hate transforms the same as love
and even a dutiful daughter can be pushed
only so far.
    When she flings his soft purse against the wall
    he bursts in a dissector's dream
    of squirming worms and mud,
    stomach, entrails, lungs,
    one small heart
    throbbing on cold stone.

Sprung from that box of green, the frog pops
out a prince, someone
she can now love.

Only his kind eyes remain a frog's
prize marbles as if to remind
change is never utterly complete:
    in the fluid hour after supper's cutlery
    and chatter, they follow the dragon-
    fly's buzzing progress
    pad to saucered pad, translucent
    wings hovering over the cool water
    like a promised kiss.
Dropped ball, the sun sinks
over the rim, his cousins' kettle chorus
riffling a shut door.

PATRICIA CARLIN

The Stepmother Arrives

The good mother sits sewing
by the window, and cries
for a daughter red as her blood,

white as the snow, black
as the window frame.
The red baby drops from her body.

Her wish is granted.
Her part is ended.
She has nothing to do but die.

The stepmother arrives.
She is carrying a mirror.
The glass child is locked inside her.

Time brightens the daughter;
the stepmother's mirror
betrays her. The boxed-in heart

of the deer will save her. But the trick
with the heart will not do forever. The stepmother
is on the trail. She knows the mirror

speaks only truth. It tells her
to change disguises.
She appears as a crone carrying an apple.

All those useless warnings.
The girl can't resist.
The ripe fruit is lodged in her body.

Weep
for her still body.
The dwarves make ready the glass coffin.

"Mother, you would never
have done this to me," she sings
in her closed glass mouth. But already

The prince spurs harder
toward her. Soon he will find her.
She has nothing to do but lie there.

His rough embrace jolts her.
The treacherous fruit
drops from her red mouth. She is open.

He carries her home to his castle. How right
that he takes her.
Days of dancing and wine will follow.

The stepmother dies
in the burning shoes. Her dancing
days are over. The girl acquires

a castle, a kingdom, a mirror,
and a new daughter.
She dances away her days in the castle.

"Mother, my glass eyes
are open," she sings
at night in her silent dream mouth.

The face in the mirror changes.
It's time for an ending.
Upstairs they are heating the iron shoes.

3

VOICES & VIEWPOINTS

grant me my generous sense of plot...

AGHA SHAHID ALI

You cannot shut me in a fairy book.

SARA HENDERSON HAY

*But I remember you before you became
a story.*

MARIE HOWE

MOYRA DONALDSON

Babe in the Woods

Each time you abandoned me, daddy,
I followed the trail back home
until I was left with nothing but crumbs.
Half of me missing, phantom.

I did not want to be lost in the dark forest,
tangled in the hair of the skinny old witch
who eats children, feeds them sweet things,
then picks at their innocence with fingers of bone.

By the time you came looking for me
I was all gone, daddy. Licked up, swallowed down.

ALLEN TATE

The Robber Bridegroom

Turn back. Turn, young lady dear
A murderer's house you enter here

I was wooed and won little bird

(I have watched them come bright girls
Out of the rising sun, with curls)
The stair is tall the cellar deep
The wind coughs in the halls

I never wish to sleep

From the ceiling the sky falls
It will press you and press you, dear.

It is my desire to fear

(What a child! she desires her fear)
The house is whirling night, the guests
Grains of dust from the northwest

I do not come for rest

There is no rest for the dead

Ready for the couch of my groom

In a long room beneath the dew
Where the walls embrace and cling.

I wear my wedding ring

He will cut off your finger
And the blood will linger

Little bird!

TIM SEIBLES

What Bugs Bunny Said to Red Riding Hood

Say, good lookin, what brings you out thisaway
amongst the fanged and the fluffy?
Grandma, huh?
Some ol bag too lazy to pick up a pot, too feeble
to flip a flapjack—
and you all dolled up like a fire engine
to cruise these woods?

This was your **mother's** idea?
She been livin in a *CrackerJack* box or somethin?
This is a tough neighborhood, mutton chops—
you gotchur badgers, your wild boar, your
hardcore grizzlies   and lately,
this one wolf's been actin pretty big and bad.

I mean, what's up, doc?
Didn anybody ever tell you it ain't smart
to stick out in wild places?
Friendly? You want friendly you better
try Detroit. I mean
you're safe wit me, sweetcakes,
but I ain't a meat-eater.

You heard about Goldie Locks, didn'cha? Well,
didn'cha? Yeah, well, little Miss Sunshine—
little Miss *I'm-so-much-cuter-than-thee*—
got caught on one of her sneaky porridge runs
and the Three Bears weren't in the mood:
so last week the game warden nabs baby bear
passin out her fingers to his pals.

That's right. Maybe your motha should
turn off her soaps, take a peek at a newspaper,
turn on some cartoons, for Pete's sake:
this woyld is about teeth, bubble buns— who's bitin
and who's gettin bit. The noyve a'that broad
sendin you out here lookin like a ripe tomata.
Why don't she just hang a sign aroun your neck:

Get over here and bite my legs off!
Cover me wit mustid—   call me a hotdawg!

Alright, alright, I'll stop.
Listen, Red, I'd hate for somethin unpleasant
to find you out here all alone.
Grandma-shmandma— let'er call *Domino's*.
They're paid to deliver. Besides, toots,
it's already later than you think—
get a load a'that chubby moon up there.

Ya can't count on Casper tanight either.
They ran that potata-head outta town two months ago—
tryin to make friends all the time—
he makes you sick after awhile.

Look, Cinderella, I got some candles and some
cold uncola back at my place— whaddaya say?

Got any artichokies in that basket?

AGHA SHAHID ALI

The Wolf's Postscript to "Little Red Riding Hood"

First, grant me my sense of history:
I did it for posterity,
for kindergarten teachers
and a clear moral:
Little girls shouldn't wander off
in search of strange flowers,
and they mustn't speak to strangers.

And then grant me my generous sense of plot:
Couldn't I have gobbled her up
right there in the jungle?
Why did I ask her where her grandma lived?
As if I, a forest-dweller,
didn't know of the cottage
under the three oak trees
and the old woman who lived there
all alone?
As if I couldn't have swallowed her years before?

And you may call me the Big Bad Wolf,
now my only reputation.
But I was no child-molester
though you'll agree she was pretty.

And the huntsman:
Was I sleeping while he snipped
my thick black fur
and filled me with garbage and stones?
I ran with that weight and fell down,
simply so children could laugh
at the noise of the stones
cutting through my belly,
at the garbage spilling out
with a perfect sense of timing,
just when the tale
should have come to an end.

LAURENCE SNYDAL

Grandmother

Inside the wolf I touched his liver with my tongue.
I wrapped my fingers all around his heart
And blessed the beat of blood. I lay me down
Between his ribs and let each sighing lung
Massage the ache from these old bones. Apart
From earth, a part of older earth, I'd grown
A snout and such big eyes and teeth so bright
They shone like sunlight. There within the cave
I called my home, I lay within his dream.
I don't remember why she lit the light.
I don't remember who she thought she'd save.
I think about the axe and want to scream.

JEAN MONAHAN

Gretel, Lost

What can we be to each other now? Before
we found the house, how brief your smile was,
but how true, how rough the collar
of the great coat we buttoned ourselves
into night after night, like twin worms
in a cocoon. The unfamiliar trail,
when you held my hand, was full of charms.
I see you at the stream, mouth like a pail:
brimming; me impatient for berries
you insist on tasting first, to see if they're
poisonous. What if there had been no house, no scary
hoots from the woods, no carrying ourselves over
that threshold with the promise of food,
a real bed? Hansel, it was good, I could see
myself growing fat with you, chopping wood,
waking up good in the gingerbread house. She
who tried to kill, she of the glazed glass and tart
apples candied to the windowsill, never meant
you harm. Her taste for life, for raw heart
on her daily plate, was just not
the way you wanted to live. By now I'll bet you see
your white cat gleaming on the roof, a wee
shaving of smoke curling out of the chimney,
are found again, home. Since you have found me
out, have seen my temper blaze, my treachery, my fire
for things not of your world, you should know that I am lost
again, in other words, myself again, the boss
of my own impossible house, who loved you
      even as I built the pyre.

REGIE CABICO

Hansel Tells Gretel of the Witch

How easy she was to please with the stories
I told through the slats of her cage.

When we stuffed our pockets with berries
and walked like ducks to fatten father's cheeks.

Or the time I thought the birds despised us
when they nibbled our bread

and left stones in our footprints.
Then nightfall and no creek to follow

all stars extinguished in the too tall branches
and whispers of stalking owls.

Stumbling when the bats fluttered sideways
round our ears till we saw

the flicker from her half-opaque windows.
Do you recall feasting off her flower pots

of chocolate and freshly baked pretzel stems,
falling asleep deep in a spell of rice pudding?

What I remember is waking to a sweat and licorice
scent. Of course I knew we'd die.

The twisted hair barrette and tattered sock,
soiled beneath my head,

were just reminders of what would come.
As she struck the match, I asked

that she not kill me or you. And in her eyes,
I saw those unforgiven ghosts.

Children like us, playing freeze tag in darkness,
charred and vanished.

From her final breath, I heard those
muffled screams, a sudden gust-like tug,

parentless and bewildered . . .
their pitch deafened by the kiln's hot hand.

MARIE HOWE

Gretel, from a sudden clearing

No way back then, you remember, we decided,
but forward, deep into a wood

so darkly green, so deafening with birdsong
I stopped my ears.

And that high chime at night,
was it really the stars, or some music

running inside our heads like a dream?
I think we must have been very tired.

I think it must have been a bad broken-off
piece at the start that left us so hungry

we turned back to a path that was gone,
and lost each other, looking.

I called your name over and over again,
and still you did not come.

At night, I was afraid of the black dogs
and often I dreamed you next to me,

but even then, you were always turning
down the thick corridor of trees.

In daylight, every tree became you.
And pretending, I kissed my way through

the forest, until I stopped pretending
and stumbled, finally, here.

Here too, there are step-parents, and bread
rising, and so many other people

you may not find me at first. They speak
your name, when I speak it.

But I remember you before you became
a story. Sometimes, I feel a thorn in my foot

when there is no thorn. They tell me,
not unkindly, that I should imagine nothing here.

But I believe you are still alive.
I want to tell you about the size of the witch

and how beautiful she is. I want to tell you
the kitchen knives only look friendly,

they have a life of their own,
and that you shouldn't be sorry,

not for the bread we ate and thought
we wasted, not for turning back alone,

and that I remember how our shadows walked
always before us, and how that was a clue,

and how there are other clues
that seem like a dream but are not,

and that every day, I am less
and less afraid.

VALERY NASH

Witch Words

I, like the children, am in the forest
and not safe
though in my gingerbread house.

I, too, am hungry.
My sugary roof and windows
no longer satisfy.
Only child flesh will fatten.

And I shiver.
Gretel, fetch axe, fetch wood.
Gretel, why are you so slow?

Over and over, it is winter:
the woodcutter, his bare larder
the wise birds choosing the crumbs
and the hunger that brings her here.

Over and over, it happens:
Gretel's daze, her dreaming step
her arms hanging down
as flat as fish.

Once again she finds me stumbling
around the rooms, half blind.
Gretel's cheeks are bright as apples.

She approaches weeping, grieving
for her caged brother, her love.
Gretel, you must light the oven.
Gretel, let me show you how.

Once again she doesn't know I planned it:
Gretel's sharp hands, her strong thrust
and afterwards, her smile.

Oh, how frightfully I howl.
The black forest rises, howls with me
roars with the fire I teach her.

SARA HENDERSON HAY

The Witch

It pleases me to give a man three wishes,
Then trick him into wasting every one.
To set the simpering goosegirl on the throne,
While the true princess weeps among the ashes.
I like to come unbidden to the christening,
Cackling a curse on the young princeling's head,
To slip a toad into the maiden's bed,
To conjure up the briers, the glass slope glistening.

And I am near, oh nearer than you've known.
You cannot shut me in a fairy book.
It was my step you heard, mine and my creatures',
Soft at your heel. And if you lean and look
Long in your mirror, you will see my features
Inextricably mingled with your own.

MAURA STANTON

The Fisherman's Wife

The fisherman said I was his third wish.
He washed off the salt, taught me to breathe,
kick my scissory legs & doze
trembling in the sharp straw beside him.
Now he had boots, a boat, a wife with gill-
silver skin who peered at the sky for fish.
I couldn't speak: The nets in my throat
trapped the shiny movements of words;
the new hands, glimmering in the dark,
only stuttered like ice across his back
while I gulped for the water! the water!
needing the density of his mouth.
When I mended sails, the needle pricked
seawater from my veins; the other wives
scurried out of their clogs for the priest
who rubbed me with garlic against the devil.
A pelican dipped & angled for my eyes—
yet I couldn't drown; the angry water
shoved me into the light, I washed inland,
shellfish clamped in my streaming hair.
The fisherman plucked leeches from my neck,
crying, "You're the last wish!" I saw torn
boots, the boat shattered on a rock.
I dreamed I was out at sea, but the shapes
went blue, blurred, I wasn't anything,
a chill, a wish, his wife stirring in sleep.

SARA HENDERSON HAY

The Sleeper

1

(*She speaks . . .*)

I wish the Prince had left me where he found me,
Wrapped in a rosy trance so charmed and deep
I might have lain a hundred years asleep.
I hate this new and noisy world around me!
The palace hums with sightseers from town,
There's not a quiet spot that I can find.
And, worst of all, he's chopped the brambles down—
The lovely briers I've felt so safe behind.

But if he thinks that with a kiss or two
He'll buy my dearest privacy, or shake me
Out of the cloistered world I've loved so long,
Or tear the pattern of my dream, he's wrong.
Nothing this clumsy trespasser can do
Will ever touch my heart, or really wake me.

2

(*He speaks . . .*)

I used to think that slumbrous look she wore,
The dreaming air, the drowsy-lidded eyes,
Were artless affectation, nothing more.
But now, and far too late, I realize
How sound she sleeps, behind a thorny wall
Of rooted selfishness, whose stubborn strands
I broke through once, to kiss her lips and hands,
And wake her heart, that never woke at all.

I wish I'd gone away that self-same hour,
Before I learned how, like her twining roses,
She bends to her own soft, implacable uses
The pretty tactics that such vines employ,
To hide the poisoned barb beneath the flower,
To cling about, to strangle, to destroy.

The Gift

Sleeping Beauty, revised

I am the thorn in everybody's side,
the feared guest. They see me
as a gift they can send back.
They have twelve gold plates and one
gold girl; I am her thirteenth
godmother, uninvited to the feast.

There's a silence in the hall
when I stride in, snow in my shawl
and lashes. There's a pinprick
in my heart until I see her, reaching
for me and laughing. Innocence
knows what comes to bless it.

Years from now, in all the tales
told, I will be the vengeful crone,
the evil fairy. They will say I struck
you from the thick weave of family
before you could bloom. In fact, your
life will be rounded with a long sleep,

a valley of charm you'll drift across.
There will be mountains beyond,
and work, the sharp work of the soul,
when you finally awake and learn
what being alive means. In time,
you'll see every other gift:

intelligence–beauty–virtue–wit:
tarnish with age and compromise.
There'll be the months when you look
into the cracked mirror of doubt and
remember the days of merrymaking
in your father's hall, that fortress of

thorns. Remember then, Briar Rose,
what I bequeath now: in place of the
ordinary spinning—suitable suitor,
suitable life—I give you a difficult
blessing, a master for whom you'll toil
to the last drop of blood through your heart:

I give you the curse of enchantment,
I give you dreams, I give you art.

CLAUDIA CARLSON

Sleeping Beauty Has Words

Did you imagine I dozed a near eternity
On a silent bed?
Under the thin linens sharp words
Pricked my skin.
All the sounds of living and dying
Troubled my sleep.

Random as: pippin, astrolabe, and plow
Full as: caul, hearth, and rye
Fool as: sonnet, quest, and joy
Sudden as: thorn, sword, and spindle
Sad as: plague, curse, and noose.

The syllables formed into dreams
As hard and daft as fate.
I lived a thousand lives!
But no grimace or smile tugged my lip.
I was the effigy of a soul
In a rose-scented room
A bas-relief in dust, mute as marble.

When the Prince gawped over me
Tumbling his words,
"Ah, sweet goddess, princess, virgin—
you and your wealth, and so on—I claim thee."
I heard his dreams.
Soft as: pupil, bride, and wife
Loud as: savior, master, and king.
He caressed crinkling satin and pristine skin,
Never sensing my heart blunt with care and sharp with use.

ANN STANFORD

The Bear

ROSE RED:
  We have once more caught
  This old humbug, sister.
  Here he lies in his shaggy coat
  Snug by our cordial fire,
  Claiming to be a prince, or a lost Christian in disguise.
  There are things of the chrysalis—the butterfly,
  Plots that must be hatched, deeds long in doing,
  But this is thorough bear, rumpled and earthen.

SNOW WHITE:
  Remember, sister, other miracles
  The pellet seed, bursting to root and leaf,
  The hard green bud to rose,
  The thought newborn
  That pecks at the skull like a rousing chick.
  Great things from small,
  The pearl from the ooze,
  And the radiant soul
  Rapt from its prison in a broken spell.

ROSE RED:
  Snakes drop their skins, but remain serpents still,
  And the moth, long harbored in its chrysalis
  Flies as a birthright to distorting flame.
  Leaves spurt from seed, but only for the season.
  No one has charted the sea-track of souls.
  Bears sleep in winter caves and wake up bears.

THE BEAR:
  The forest offers honey, hollow logs,
  Streams fraught with fishes,
  Berries on the hills.
  Yet here I ponder.
  I am no common bear, for I have visions.

I dreamed I was a prince—
I walked in halls
Clanging with armor;
Underneath this pelt
I feel the hardness of the golden mail.
Can such dissatisfaction offer proof
I am enmeshed in spells too fine to ravel?

Snow White, Rose Red, divert your clumsy wooer.
Some day we meet the dwarf and force the answer.

DEBORA GREGER

Snow White and Rose Red

The bear at the door, begging
to be beaten free of his snowy coat,
was a king's son under a curse,
detail my sister and I learned long after

we scoured him with brooms and then lay down,
pale crescents pinned to his vast dark.
Rose claimed that in firelight
his fur glittered but I saw no more

than before, when a coin warmed in my hand
pressed a queen's profile into the ice
coiled in fronds against the window.
In the eye-size opening melted tear by cool tear,

had I seen something break from the forest's deep ranks?
I saw nothing beyond an animal knowing—
if it be knowing—what a lost hunter does:
on such a night any warmth will do.

So in the heart of a wood a man will sleep
inside the beast he's slain, waiting daybreak
to illumine the way toward any clearing.
Toward a cottage like the one where red roses

and white clambered to the window,
the sanguine and the snowflake's distant kin
spendthrift with promise of good company
as they vied for my sister's shears.

In a cut-glass vase too fine for the rough table
on which lay bread and books for two,
a bouquet would hold its salon
while as always we rudely, mutely read—

Rose, someone's travels bound in red morocco;
I, botany of the season ahead
where *naked* meant *without specialized scales*
and *tender: not enduring winter,*

the author looking out for those
after his own heart—*If it is too cold
to read in the field, save this
for the warmth of home.*

Shadows unroll across the bluing snow
but enough oblique light has pierced
a man-made pond gracing the palace grounds
that, out of a slow internal melting,

ice crystals regrow into bloom and thorn
as men harvest them, sawing the water
into frozen bales, loading sledges
tomorrow will drag to the icehouse.

The tree overlooking this—is it weeping?
Not markedly weeping.
Are the leaf scars solitary?
There are two or more at each node.

The bear, that long lost night?
He was one of two brothers.
One picked Rose to wed,
the one who had been animal chose me.

Wind rattles a fist of milkweed
until it's prized open, loosing a handful
of tufted halfpennies one by one,
that each be borne far off and root where it falls.

DAVID TRINIDAD

Rapunzel

for Sharon Smith

Like hair, the days and nights are growing longer
    and longer.
Nothing interests me. The landscape's flat: paths and
    dry fields,
villages, the same tiered orchard. My thick tresses
    twist, spread
down, surround me like the moat at the foot of this
    tower
in which I wait and waste my thoughts. The stone keeps
    cold, corners
dark; cobwebs as abandoned as the lace above my
    breasts.

Flies multiply on split fruit-skins in a wooden bowl
    next
to the barred window. Dust layers stream in. The sun
    lowers.

And each evening, the crone comes. Her crackled fingers
    appear
pinching the key. She brings round loaves of stale bread
    and water.
Carefully, she clasps my throat, lifts my face in front
    of her
like a hand-mirror, moans, weeps. If only once she'd say:
    "Here,
take this pair of scissors and cut your hair before it
    twists
into spaces between the bricks like vines." I'd slit my
    wrists.

LISA RUSS SPAAR

Rapunzel Shorn

I'm redeemed, head light
as seed mote, as a fasting
girl's among these thorns, lips
and fingers bloody with fruit.
Years I dreamed of this:
the green, laughing arms
of old trees extended over me,
my shadow lost among theirs.
Where is my severed ladder,
the empty tower of my hair?
Let the birds fall in love
with it, carry it away.
Here on earth the river
is in love with itself.
To get there, I'll shove
sharp stones into my shoes
as the saints did, lest
I forget what it means
to walk again upon it.

GWEN STRAUS

The Prince

Imagine this: we're in the garden harvesting,
and you're telling me how our children suckled,
Their mouths opened like dark moons.

When you speak to me like this,
I want you to say everything,
and I want to put my hands on your lips
while you say it.

For a long time I was blind,
even before the thorns of roses tattered my eyes.
I was bored, handsome, a Prince.
The thrill was in what I could get away with.

For the entanglement of arms, legs, hair, I called out,
Rapunzel, like a hammer and a saw.
Now I say your name over and over,
a deep humming river. I am an old man in love,

which is not the same thing as a young Prince
adventuring. After I fell from your tower
I wandered through tangled forests,
through the scramble of first frost,
then snow, then false spring. I had changed
and could not return to my father's kingdom.

Imagine this: in the dark, I see your body
with my hands; the soft slack skin of your belly,
the blue hollow behind your ears, your boyish
cropped hair. For days we smile silly.
Sometimes I catch you smiling like that to the spinach.

All my childhood I heard about love
but I thought only witches could grow it
in gardens behind walls too high to climb.

I travelled through blindness
like doubt, with its huge devouring mouth.
The kiss of fern brushed my ankles.
The loamy smell of mushrooms and loss
clung to my fingers. I learned how to cry.

And then you were there,
washing clear my thorn-scratched eyes.
Our skin touching is soft, a baby.
If I were to ask how you grew a garden
in this wasteland, you would say,
A river of tears and a desert's patience.

PENELOPE SHUTTLE

Ashputtel

(*Cinderella*)

My face is black with ashes,
I can see nothing
though I hear the near-silence
and nostalgia of my father's fountains,
smell far off the festive bonfires.
It is pain without salves,
my body is metal,
slapped across my shoulders
I'll ring like a gong.
If there are treasures in this dark,
I cannot hope to carry them off,
I know I'm uglier than my sisters,
will turn any beholder to stone.
Must I sit here forever,
tethered, homeless,
or dare I ask for a diet of light,
a shining nourishment,
rinse off my blindness,
see above me in their prosperous palaces
my sisters, my million sisters, the stars;
My Vanessas and Sophias,
suffer them to pour their nymphean pitchers
over me, clothing me
head to foot in their clean threshed glitters,
guipure of starlight at my hem,
crochet of moonstone and pearl at my throat,
my bodice and skirt whiter than the lace aprons of my stepsisters,
my gloves woven from the first memory of silk,
at my breast an unbarterable diamond;

feel again my stockinged-feet slipping into sandals that shine?

BRUCE BENNETT

Straw Into Gold

The Miller's Daughter

It was my father who claimed I could spin straw
into gold, I who can barely thread a needle.

Since then it's one damned room after another,
with the attentions of a midget.

If I'm lucky, they say, I'll marry the King, a bore
who'd just as soon kill me.

Why didn't he brag I'm beautiful and a virgin?
At least I'd have had a night on the town.

Rumplestiltskin

If I play this right, I'll get her and the baby both.
She'll have to tell how she turned all that straw into
gold, and he'll boot them out. That's the sort of pig
he is. Call me runt, will he? And she's another. Two of
a kind, they are. Games? She doesn't know what games
are. Just wait till she and the kid are in my house in
the woods. Then they'll see games.

The King

Gold, gold, glorious gold! Heaps and heaps
turned into gold! I'll build them high as mountains.
I'll impound the harvest. I'll have straw imported!
Death to anyone who touches a piece of straw!

The Miller

That little slut! Imagine, keeping a secret like that!
From her father! I'd'a whipped her good. And I'd'a
kept my mouth shut; you can bet on that! She'd'a spun
night and day. In a couple months, I'd'a been King.

Imagine!

That little slut!

GWEN STRAUS

Her Shadow

Straw burning into gold
smells of rotten eggs
with a hint of lemons and almonds.

Those trinkets—
my mother's wedding ring, her necklace,
they were gifts from my father.
I gave them to him as easily
as my father had given me,
one day on the way to market, boasting.

I would have done anything
for his company in the heaps of straw,
his pimpled face, his songs. I liked his size,
and even his ugliness. We played puns
and riddles while he spun. When he asked
for my child, what did I care for the King's child?

I didn't know then how a baby
can have nothing to do with the father
when it falls asleep in your arms
smelling of sweet-sour milk.

When he came again,
I had not forgotten our time
in the dim room of wheels,
how he woke me with the tender tickling
of straw behind my ears.
The King has never touched me that way.

But I was ashamed and it was easier to despise him.
On the third day he arrived smelling faintly of beer
and baking bread, jovial, less lonely.
He gave back the ring. Then I said his name
and he pulled one leg until he split apart, in front of us.
Since then, I have felt old.

He tore himself in two, for me,
like a shadow, asking for my golden-haired child,
the seed of another man.

SUSAN THOMAS

Snow White in Exile

Mother, I dream of dragonflies
and insect wings, the furry undersides
of bats. I dream of poison figs
and silver spiders. I dream of you
in your tower, stirring potions
to preserve your famous beauty.
The little men don't know
that every time I let you in
it's not because you trick me,
but that I hope you'll take me home.

But Mother, I know what happens.
I've seen it in your mirror: the poison apple
locked in my throat, the ugly grieving dwarves,
the prince who brings me back to life
with ardent, sloppy kisses.
And Mother, I know my joyous
and terrible wedding day.
The iron slippers lie ready.
They'll force them on your pretty feet.
You will dance for us and die.

Mother, I'll dream for all my life
of spells, infusions, nightshade,
entrails in glass jars, ground beetles,
not of the mother who wished me
white as snow and red as blood,
and died when I was born.
I'll dream of your hand in mine
as we climb the tower stairs.
I'll dream of the smiling mirror
and your sweet breath
kissing my cheek like a feather.

MARTIN MOONEY

Dwarves

for Moyra Donaldson

Whether we came of our own free will hey ho or were driven
    no one remembers
we live inhospitably, tending forges and mines, doing
    our own housework
some are so stunted and ugly the rest of us laugh or retch
    but in general
we try to ignore how we look and restrain ourselves
    to workmanlike barks
"shovel," "pickaxe," "diamond," "soup," that sort of thing
    and the very notion
of torrents of song at the start of or end of or during
    a hard day's work
is something we'd frown on

                    so when she arrived
    at our barracks
sweeping and crooning, her notions of food and deportment
    so courtly, so gentle,
so in a word tall hey ho embarrassed us greatly
    we shrank from her laugh
staying up late to prepare food we'd actually eat
    and after a shift
we'd compete to avoid elocution, classes in tact
    for the taciturn
and the handstitched finery she so obsessively wove us
    we the illiterate
learned at her side hey ho to despise themselves
    the grossly deformed
to despise their uglier comrades

                    so we were relieved
    to discover her body
stretched in a clearing under our barracks window
    the nugget of apple
still lodged at the root of her discoloured tongue
    no one went near her

for hours, then some of us built her a coffin of glass
    for now she was dead
we wanted to study this wonder of civilised life, to stare
    at its beauty and not
risk a homily, one of her gentle correctives
    we would never be happy
again, now we'd been shown the impossible shape
    of a life not ours
but hauling our shame to the pit at dawn the following day
    some of us sang

KIMIKO HAHN

Fervor

I killed my half brother—
shaking him in his sleep his head
fell off his blue body.
I'm sorry, I shouted. I'm really
sorry. You try living
with the sight of a purplish neck bone
or surprised eyes open towards you.
And now he is a blue bird
tiny as a child's heart, ardent
as a man's. He pecks my lips,
spots my smock.
Amazing how far an apology will go.

4 ∾

SPELL BINDING &
SPELL BREAKING

It is part of the spell
STEVIE SMITH

And yet, it was not real.
ANN STANFORD

held
In the crystalline moment of time stopped,
HAYDEN CARRUTH

ALASTAIR REID

A Spell for Sleeping

Sweet william, silverweed, sally-my-handsome.
Dimity darkens the pittering water.
On gloomed lawns wanders a king's daughter.
Curtains are clouding the casement windows.
A moon-glade smurrs the lake with light.
Doves cover the tower with quiet.

Three owls whit-whit in the withies.
Seven fish in a deep pool shimmer.
The princess moves to the spiral stair.

Slowly the sickle moon mounts up.
Frogs hump under moss and mushroom.
The princess climbs to her high hushed room,

Step by step to her shadowed tower.
Water laps the white lake shore.
A ghost opens the princess' door.

    Seven fish in the sway of the water.
    Six candles for a king's daughter.
    Five sighs for a drooping head.
    Four ghosts to gentle her bed.
    Three owls in the dusk falling.
    Two tales to be telling.
    One spell for sleeping.

Tamarisk, trefoil, tormentil.
Sleep rolls down from the clouded hill.
A princess dreams of a silver pool.

The moonlight spreads, the soft ferns flitter.
Stilled in a shimmering drift of water,
Seven fish dream of a king's lost daughter.

HAYDEN CARRUTH

from *The Sleeping Beauty*

4

Three persons are here, of whom the first
Is *you,* dear princess, you who are always sleeping,
Thou therefore addressed—
Thou in thy quiet-keeping—
As if immutably; and yet you dream. You rest
And you dream this world. You are mystery. You exist.

Second is *he,* the prince. He lives
Wherever and whenever he perceives
Himself in your dreaming, though in fact he is awake
And so knows the horror of being
Only a dream.

           Third is the poem, who must make
Presence from words, vision from seeing,
This no one that uniquely in sorrow rejoices
And can have no pronoun.

           Last, as in all dreaming,
Is heard the echo of coincidental voices.

48

Dornröschen, princess
    are not you too   held
In the crystalline moment of time stopped,
    you lying
So demurely propped,   naked and spelled,
On the couch of stone/
               The purifying
Of icy fire surrounds you/
                  Beyond it, quelled
Forever, is the what-might-have-been, for you,
    though the unimpelled,
Are the dreamer whose significant dreaming
Still brings,   dream by dream,   the seeming
That will be the world/
             You lie in the center,
The integration
And the nowhereness of all things,
    as seasons of being turn
    around the winter/
O northern princess,
          see these apparitions,
How they gather in dreams, our history from the mist,
The meaningless, mysterious images of your dreaming
    reason
That you will know
          the instant you are really kissed.

115

In wavering shadow and silted with soot, her face
Seems as if almost dreaming, as if under water,
Where she lies in one more ruined place
In this history of the Slaughter
Of the Innocents. How beautiful. The disgrace
Of love's civility riven like the lace
From her own breast, of death and pain
And lamentation and blood, the stain
Contaminating all the bright world she has made
Seem not to touch her.
He gazes down at her, insane, afraid,
For this will be the end. Never
Will our world lie again in her dream's keeping.
He bends to her, the real and loving other.
She wakes,
        sees,
              screams.
                        She begins her weeping.

SUE OWEN

The Glass Coffin

Now you sleep
the pretty death.
Snow White, the poisoned
apple you bit is
caught in your throat.

Snow White, your body
is like your name now,
thick with a cold
that grips you.
Your blue eyes return no
knowing when looked in.

You must be dreaming
that blankness of winter.
Snow White,
it must be a place
of few stars and great
air, where movement is
always only a wind.

And your two hands, that
cannot remember what
they held, must lie
empty like birds' nests.
Your arms emptied
themselves of holding too,
like trees that drop
their bleeding leaves.

Snow White, you
are a child of sleep and
loneliness.
The days come and breath
steps its way, slowly,
through you, because
someone wants you and will
melt your lips of ice.

DENISE DUHAMEL

Sleeping Beauty's Dreams

One hundred years is a long time
to sleep. The whirling spinning wheels
with loose cord bands bouncing like dangerous bicycle chains.
The popping bobbins and evil spindles,
lethal injections. Counting backwards,
she sees inventions way beyond her own future.
The modern sewing machine with spool pins
and presser foot, thread guides and a button
for reverse feed. The needle, up and down,
repeats, like sex, like sex with the Prince
who hasn't woken her yet.
Changing fashions from ruffles to miniskirts.
Running water from silver animal snouts.
Time sways as horizontal as she lies.
History spills from a ripped vacuum cleaner bag.
She sucks up the dirt from a rug. She gets a shock
from a frayed cord. Her girl and boy, Dawn and Day, run
to meet their clairvoyant parent.
Her mother-in-law is a queen ogre. The Prince, a wimp.
Her children's grandmother wants to eat them.
Her own mother and father are dead. The fairies,
the world's kindness, flit through landscapes
trying to make things right. A cook will substitute
a deer for Sleeping Beauty, and the ogre will lick her plate.
The Prince will not be the one to save her in the end.
He'll be away, off fighting a war. Walt Disney
is frozen in a tank next to her. The river
and the road, cryogenics and the coma.
Scrub boards melt into washing machines.
Someone stitches her eyes shut,
but she doesn't bleed. Her pricked finger
oozes gold. She hurdles over an ironing board.
She's kissing her dead father when the Prince kisses her awake.
Groggy, she looks for infinity through his eyes,
dark and small like dustpans' hang holes.

STEVIE SMITH

The Frog Prince

I am a frog,
I live under a spell,
I live at the bottom
Of a green well.

And here I must wait
Until a maiden places me
On her royal pillow,
And kisses me,
In her father's palace.

The story is familiar,
Everybody knows it well,
But do other enchanted people feel as nervous
As I do? The stories do not tell,

Ask if they will be happier
When the changes come,
As already they are fairly happy
In a frog's doom?

I have been a frog now
For a hundred years
And in all this time
I have not shed many tears,

I am happy, I like the life,
Can swim for many a mile
(When I have hopped to the river)
And am for ever agile.

And the quietness,
Yes, I like to be quiet
I am habituated
To a quiet life,

But always when I think these thoughts,
As I sit in my well
Another thought comes to me and says:
It is part of the spell

To be happy
To work up contentment
To make much of being a frog
To fear disenchantment

Says, It will be *heavenly*
To be set free,
Cries, *Heavenly* the girl who disenchants
And the royal times, *heavenly*,
And I think it will be.

Come, then, royal girl and royal times,
Come quickly,
I can be happy until you come
But I cannot be heavenly,
Only disenchanted people
Can be heavenly.

SUSAN WHEELER

Fractured Fairy Tale

So activate then. Beforehand the birds
settle in for a roost, and the shiny clock hands
start to rattle. The frog prince bewails
his casaba schnozz. *De*-activate's more like it.

Several men rest their rakes at their crotches and begin to talk.
They are having an ur-argument. They are arguing over
pure and impure analyticity, or error theory or a nonfactualist
theory about ethics. It might be the Chinese Room Argument.
The light through the elms reminds them of dinner.
The hunger reminds them of loss.

Doze Doll Does Wiz Biz—a century that, her sleeping,
a stenotic century self-circling, noodling in its tunes, drug
by the scuff of its kitchen to stand, squinting, at *thing*
coherent, drooping from clouds, bungeeing to boot.

ANN STANFORD

The Sleeping Princess

I don't remember when I fell asleep,
Half up the stair, or dropped from a summer hill,
Or yawning into bedtime. But the dream
So counterfeited me, I could not tell

I was asleep. For in that sleep the sun
Shone on my eyes, I rose and breathed the day,
Widened the doors, ran to the summer lawn,
And spent the seasons prodigal as snow.

Still I was careful. There the sleeper lay.
I took such journeys as were possible.
My diary was complete, and it could show
Much was accomplished, and the days turned full.

And yet it was not real. I find the book
Dusty, unwritten in. For someone called
And touched my cheek. The spendthrift years were done.
Was it a kiss? I woke. And I was old.

LUCILLE CLIFTON

sleeping beauty

when she woke up
she was terrible.
under his mouth her mouth
turned red and warm
then almost crimson as the coals
smothered and forgotten
in the grate.
she had been gone so long.
there was much to unlearn.
she opened her eyes.
he was the first thing she saw
and she blamed him.

ANNA RABINOWITZ

Beauty Sleeping Now

So you wait, so you wait,

One hundred years you trance,
Marrow smoldering in your bones,
While queen and king, commoner
And knight snore decades' snores

And winters turn
And then return
To nothing new.

Silence stokes the great stone halls,
The fire's home is ash, and comatose,
You're dead alive
Until the prince lopes in.

But this time your eyes fly open
Before Charming plants his kiss upon your lips,

And when His Highness bends
To pluck you from your sleep,
Oh, Beauty, how he withers
As you trap his tongue between your teeth.

SHARON DOLIN

Jealousy

after Jealousy,
a painting by Howard Hodgkin

Squares of burning sienna guard
an inner courtyard of lettuces

      moving you toward and away
      from a heart of burning reticence
      that soon became a mode of self—
      a defining mood of petulance

to break the spell
      peer down
      the round-by-round
      stairwell

until you get so dizzy you see
these walls you've built, your russet ire
let down Rapunzel let down
is the wood that stokes

her golden-haired fire.

MURIEL RUKEYSER

Fable

for Herbert Kohl

Yes it was the prince's kiss.
But the way was prepared for the prince.
It had to be.

When the attendants carrying the woman
—dead they thought her lying on the litter—
stumbled over the root of a tree
the bit of deathly apple in her throat
jolted free.

Not strangled, not poisoned!
She
can come alive.

It was an "accident" they hardly noticed.

The threshold here comes when they stumble.
The jolt. And better if we notice,
However, their noticing is not
Essential to the story.

A miracle has even deeper roots,
Something like error, some profound defeat.
Stumbled-over, the startle, the arousal,
Something never perceived till now, the taproot.

LISEL MUELLER

Immortality

In Sleeping Beauty's castle
the clock strikes one hundred years
and the girl in the tower returns to the
world.
So do the servants in the kitchen,
who don't even rub their eyes.
The cook's right hand, lifted
an exact century ago,
completes its downward arc
to the kitchen boy's left ear;
the boy's tensed vocal cords
finally let go
the trapped, enduring whimper,
and the fly, arrested mid-plunge
above the strawberry pie,
fulfills its abiding mission
and dives into the sweet, red glaze.

As a child I had a book
with a picture of that scene.
I was too young to notice
how fear persists, and how
the anger that causes fear persists,
that its trajectory can't be changed
or broken, only interrupted.
My attention was on the fly:
that this slight body
with its transparent wings
and lifespan of one human day
still craved its particular share
of sweetness, a century later.

5

MAGICAL
OBJECTS

*the power to transform
is theirs—*

ELAINE EQUI

*most whimsical
and harmless at first...*

LISA RUSS SPAAR

ELAINE EQUI

The Objects in Fairy Tales

are always
the most important
characters.
Then as now,
the power to transform
is theirs—
the story
a way of talking through
(and to) us.
Shoes of Fortune,
Magic Beans,
are unlike objects
in magazines
for they awaken
us against our will
from the spell of abject
longing for more.
Only then do we live
happily ever after.

2.

They speak
but not
to everyone,

just those
ready to hear
and endure

what they have to say—

impossible tasks,

shine wrapped around
the seedvoice.

Golden apples
in the grasp of time.

"I'll climb up."

3.

(we are)
            Forever turning

things into thoughts

or caught mid-air
dangling between

the way children
steep their toys
in imagination.

A bird's heart
in him.

Clouds will catch
and carry him off.

4.

But finally, the objects
in fairy tales are words.

Beautiful as any object
we re-call

"water"
            "daughter"

Gazing down
in the cellar
through the window
to the face,

Then the tall man
made a ring of himself,

flames
trembling like cold,

old skirt
        old stockings—

pride and arrogance.

"If you stretch yourself
you'll be there
in a couple of steps."

ALICE FRIMAN

Snow White: The Mirror

Even after she left
to follow her necessity—stepping through
her ritual of trial, I held her
in the locket of my frame.

She never spoke of it, but knew
for she in her child way would stare at me
then slip her long white dress
unbraid the black silk rope of hair
and stand—her budding snow
            fluttering the edges of the dark.

She sought like Psyche to see the face of Love
and I her only candle:

            Mirror, Mirror on the wall
            Who is the fairest of them all?

That I, trembling, brimmed the silver legend
of my heart and gave her back
the sight she gave to me.

Sometimes even now on snow white nights
when the moon spills her name across the floor
I think I hear her footstep on the stair
and in the silver jelly of my eye
light, so she might see, the votive candle
then float the only constant I have known:

My own white girl. My snow narcissus. Crown.

ANNE SHELDON

Snow White Turns 39

I'm planning how to break a talking mirror:
hammer and earplugs. Seven years of bad luck?
Better than that Bette Davis cackle
every morning when I hit the sink
without my make-up. One black dawn, I'll raise
my cheekbones to the light and all those watts
will fail to flush away these tear-track shadows.
Then I will smash the Glass. And take up chess.
No more clipping recipes for sautéed
hearts of virgin, I can tell you that,
or sending milkmaids out to feed the wolves.
No more wolves to feed, or woodsmen, either,
in our tidy kingdom. My husband found me
under glass. How I miss the woodsman.

SUE OWEN

The Poisoned Apple

Snow White, I want
to explain everything
from this green
tree where I still hang
on the bough.

I want you to know
that this shape I am
is what the sun taught.
I had to learn this
trick of shine, this red
that is my destiny.

Neither you nor I
know why the wind whispers
about a mirror that
tries to lie, or can
imagine a story we could
make up about jealousy.

But I know one day,
a ladder and a hand
could come to pick me.
Any queen who wanted to
take me, because
she hates, could dip my
one-half into a poison.

It is fate that my
prettiness and sweetness
will draw someone close,
until the bite.
I want to explain this
now, if I am that
apple, that red period
that will stop your life.

NATASHA SAJÉ

Rampion

Let us praise this most polynomial
of plants: In English it's lamb's lettuce,
named perhaps for the delicate ear
or tonguelike leaves.
Imagine a small cat's paw
or a spoon for demitasse.
We also call it corn salad,
growing as it does protected
from the sun between stalks.
The French say *mâche*
but also *blanchette* (little white)
clairette (little light)
doucette (little soft)
oreillette (little ear).
In Latin, it's *valerian*,
akin to catnip, the bellflower
whose medicinal roots prevent spasms.
One pays dearly for this plant
because it's hard to clean, demanding
a large tub of cool water and someone
to lift it slowly
many times, spurning
the grass and grains of sand.
But worth the trouble for its leaves smooth
as mayonnaise, colored
like clover, flavored of walnuts.
To some it's salad, to others
it's a fairy tale. The stuff
Rapunzel's mother craved
and that the old witch grew and guarded.
The stuff an unborn child is bartered for.
It recalls the persistence of desire.

LISA RUSS SPAAR

Rapunzel's Clock

Of all the gifts he could have brought her
that she would seem to have no use for
in the tower—a lawnmower, badminton set,
high-heeled shoes—
this clock was most whimsical
and harmless at first, a toy house
carved with vines, flaunting a frozen bird
that popped in and out, and was always
whisked away at the last chime,
back through clenched doors,
as though to store up the intervening hour
in undistracted darkness.
After a night of counting every hour,
they destroyed the clock's music
to keep it secret from the Crone,
though at night, while he slept,
she could still hear its lurching gears,
the tongue-less bird shuttling its muted cuckoos
inside the cupboard where she kept it hidden.
It became the tight heart
she tuned her body to—
the crumbs of afternoons, his absences,
the gaining dark. Blood days.
Days of waiting. Nights of visitation
and violent blooming.
So that in time she grew to need
the clock's white noise
beneath her own body's story—
its given loneliness, its brief,
incredible eruptions of hope.

JANE SHORE

The Glass Slipper

The little hand was on the eight.
It scoured Cinderella's face, radiant
since her apotheosis; blue dress,
blonde page-boy curled like icing on a cake.
The wristwatch came packed in a glass slipper
—really plastic, but it looked like glass—
like one of my mother's shoes, but smaller.
High transparent heel, clear shank and sole,
it looked just big enough to fit me.

I stuffed my left foot halfway in,
as far as it would go.
But when I limped across the bedroom rug,
the slipper cut its outline
into my swelling heel.
No matter which foot I tried,
I couldn't fit the ideal
that marks the wearer's virtue,
so I went about my business
of being good. If I was good enough,
in time the shoe might fit.
I cleaned my room, then polished
the forepaws of the Georgian chair;
while in the kitchen, squirming in her high chair,
a bald and wizened empress on her throne,
my baby sister howled one red vowel
over and over.

Beside the white mulch of the bedspread,
my parents' Baby Ben wind-up alarm
was three minutes off.
Each night, its moonface,
a luminous and mortuary green,
guided me between my parents' sleeping forms
where I slept
until the mechanism of my sister's hunger,
accurate as quartz,

woke my mother and me moments before
the alarm clock sprang my father to the sink
and out the door.

Seven forty-five. His orange Mercury
cut a wake of gravel in the driveway.
Like a Chinese bride I hobbled after him,
nursing my sore foot in a cotton sock.
Cinderella's oldest sister lopped off
her own big toe with a kitchen knife
to make the slipper fit, and her middle sister
sliced her heel down to size.
Even the dumbstruck Prince failed to notice
while ferrying to the palace
each of his false fiancées,
the blood filling her glass slipper.
The shoehorn's silver tongue
consoled each one in turn,
"When *you* are Queen, you won't *need* to walk."

The Twelve Dancing Princesses

Seen so far, so high above the legend
As spiral nebulae glittering but misted
They shake their light-year hair,
Their narrow feet in pearls step into clouds,
They arch their royal palms
Revolving away from time, whirled by a music
Only for twenty-four ears—
Even the chanted princes cannot sway to their sound.

Yet they exist, having come down to us
As twelve, as princesses, as dancers where
The turns of viols push their sudden shadows over water.

Some of us might say
Thank the old woman, if you love them, and her short cloak
Or the poor soldier, and his wound, and sponge:
But they no more, being over-ground, than under,
Bring us their dozen blossoms shaped of air.
Thank lakeside castle, lit by joyous drums,
Which gave them floor and built such saraband!
But it's *all* magical.
Therefore, unreliable.

Not so, their silken shoes.

If in the morning their shoes had not been frayed,
If in the morning (under gilt beds)
Damp from the avenues of jewelled trees,
The holes of trumpets blown through fabric soles
Earth stained, earth stained!—
We never would have known.

Therefore the daughters' motion, and the little boats
Perhaps that carried them, wink into sight
By virtue of *desire*. They wanted to dance. In natural shoes.

BARBARA CROOKER

Masquerade

Ladies' slippers bloom:
pouchy satin on waxy roots,
but no one now wears dancing shoes.

The ball is over, Cinderella,
the stars are blown out.
The prince wears velvet sneakers,
a media man, his glossy
image tacked on every tree.

Glass cuts deep in your veins
when your life is spent dancing
to the ragged beat of the band.
The matched pearls grow cold
on your windpipe; the cummerbund
reticulates and swallows
to the rhythm of the dance.

It's past midnight now, tired lady.
The pink slippers glow in the dark,
spent weapons of the betrayers.
The black velvet night is all you need
on your bare damask skin.

RUSSELL EDSON

Cinderella's Life at the Castle

After Cinderella married the prince she turned her attention to minutiae, using her glass slipper as a magnifying lens.

When at court she would wear orange peels and fish tins, and other decorous rubbish as found in back of the castle.

You are making me very nervous, said the prince.

But Cinderella continued to look at something through her glass slipper.

Did you hear me? said the prince.

Cinderella's mouth hung open as she continued to look at something through her glass slipper.

Did you hear me, did you hear me, did you hear me? screamed the prince.

6

DESIRE & ITS DISCONTENTS

to love on, oh yes...
GALWAY KINNELL

and love's a hard word...
ALIKI BARNSTONE

A forbidden fruit to make us wise
ALICE FRIMAN

CAROL ANN DUFFY

Little Red-Cap

At childhood's end, the houses petered out
into playing fields, the factory, allotments
kept, like mistresses, by kneeling married men,
the silent railway line, the hermit's caravan,
till you came at last to the edge of the woods.
It was there that I first clapped eyes on the wolf.

He stood in a clearing, reading his verse out loud
in his wolfy drawl, a paperback in his hairy paw,
red wine staining his bearded jaw. What big ears
he had! What big eyes he had! What teeth!
In the interval, I made quite sure he spotted me,
sweet sixteen, never been, babe, waif, and bought me a drink,

my first. You might ask why. Here's why. Poetry.
The wolf, I knew, would lead me deep into the woods,
away from home, to a dark tangled thorny place
lit by the eyes of owls. I crawled in his wake,
my stockings ripped to shreds, scraps of red from my blazer
snagged on twig and branch, murder clues. I lost both shoes

but got there, wolf's lair, better beware. Lesson one that night,
breath of the wolf in my ear, was the love poem.
I clung till dawn to his thrashing fur, for
what little girl doesn't dearly love a wolf?
Then I slid from between his heavy matted paws
and went in search of a living bird—white dove—

which flew, straight, from my hands to his open mouth.
One bite, dead. How nice, breakfast in bed, he said,
licking his chops. As soon as he slept, I crept to the back
of the lair, where a whole wall was crimson, gold, aglow with books.
Words, words were truly alive on the tongue, in the head,
warm, beating, frantic, winged; music and blood.

But then I was young—and it took ten years
in the woods to tell that a mushroom

stoppers the mouth of a buried corpse, that birds
are the uttered thought of trees, that a greying wolf
howls the same old song at the moon, year in, year out,
season after season, same rhyme, same reason. I took an axe

to a willow to see how it wept. I took an axe to a salmon
to see how it leapt. I took an axe to the wolf
as he slept, one chop, scrotum to throat, and saw
the glistening, virgin white of my grandmother's bones.
I filled his old belly with stones. I stitched him up.
Out of the forest I come with my flowers, singing, all alone.

ALICE FRIMAN

Rapunzel

When he saw her singing in his dreams
  her hair like lofty hay
   bulging out the window slits
he called
and she, braided in his silver voice
let down the golden line.

If she was unwise about such things
that girls are taught: of men
  with chocolate kisses
  who offer lifts to lessons,
  who stand too close in subways
  playing with their change
then what was he?
Caught in that small room,
the braid
coiling the floorboards like a snake,
and she all Rubens-ripe and curious.

Oh, the tower-singing on that wheezy couch.
Forbidden fruits in platters of her flesh
and he, with scars to touch along his side
and many wondrous things to name.
     Until, like hair,
undone, they slept inside that nest
  fledglings on an apple bough
  all golden delicious.

What's this of guilt and fall?
A forbidden fruit to make us wise,
the bitter sin of Sundays?

They coupled in a cave
or on a bank in Eden.
Let us hope (for art)
the stars were out that night
and tigers padded softly in the bush.

BRUCE BENNETT

The Skeptical Prince

He thinks he caught a glimpse once; heard a song.
But that was long ago. He could be wrong.
He'd scale the tower, burst the bonds, he'll swear,
if she'll just give some token she is there.

The town has grown accustomed to the sight:
he drinks by day, then hangs around at night,
purveying sad and antiquated lore,
insisting he will act once he is sure.

His horse is stabled elsewhere. He'll decide,
he claims, the day, the hour, he will ride.
He's waiting for a sign. He wants it known
his purpose holds. And he'll not leave alone.

CLAUDIA CARLSON

Rumplestiltskin Keeps Mum

He was able to make hay into ore.
He was able to make peasant into queen.
He was not able to make rise the rumpled
skin between his parenthetic legs.
As if he ever needed her insignificant dowry.
Amber beads? Her little ring? No, he needed
someone to teach the lexicon he knew;
a student, a scribe, an heir, this infant son
codified in royal flesh.

He's keeping mum.
Let her ask, his name is buried.

The power in names is well documented.
Rosetta stone junkies and the code breakers,
all those efforts at making a key
turn when he, he was ready to stop

turning. Too weary, too lame, his past
misquoted and plagiarized,
he was now Mr. Anonymous.
He had read the scrolls and hieroglyphs.
He knew the cliff where the phoenix rose.
He picked the herbs a hedgewitch picks.
The libraries of Alexandria still burned in his eyes.
Let other men tear bindings, pillage
language, spread words like fleas.
Let women grunt their syllables of forcing
new souls to repeat the words of the world.

He'd never tell,
He's keeping mum.

GALWAY KINNELL

Kissing the Toad

Somewhere this dusk
a girl puckers her mouth
and considers kissing
the toad a boy has plucked
from the cornfield and hands
her with both hands;
rough and lichenous
but for the immense ivory belly,
like those old entrepreneurs
sprawling on Mediterranean beaches,
with popped eyes,
it watches the girl who might kiss it,
pisses, quakes, tries
to make its smile wider:
to love on, oh yes, to love on.

ANNA DENISE

How to Change a Frog Into a Prince

Start with the underwear. Sit him down.
Hopping on one leg may stir unpleasant memories.
If he gets his tights on, even backwards, praise him.
Fingers, formerly webbed, struggle over buttons.
Arms and legs, lengthened out of proportion, wait,
as you do, for the rest of him to catch up.
This body, so recently reformed, reclaimed,
still carries the marks of its time as a frog. Be gentle.
Avoid the words awkward and gawky.
Do not use tadpole as a term of endearment.
His body, like his clothing, may seem one size too big.
Relax. There's time enough for crowns. He'll grow into it.

JEANNE MARIE BEAUMONT

Where's Wolf?

Where are you, my wild, my hazard, my gilded eye?
With your ears like inside-out peaches, your tongue
        a washcloth's linen.
I've brought you merlot in the picnic basket you loved
        to pick through,
I've brought you cranberries, recalling how lavishly
        you licked their juice from my thumbs.
This was the path where we agreed to rendezvous,
        this the pine.
I'm easy to spot, my lips in Ruby Butter gloss,
        I'm on time.

I met a man in town who resembles you but
        too salon-sleek,
without your mossy smell, your silent feet.
He sent carnations round to mother's place.
I won't settle for mannered inoffensiveness.
I want moon-witnessed trysts, wind battling
        my body, the bed of needles, bark.
The rogue happiness we captured once.
O where o where have you hidden since?

MARTHA CARLSON-BRADLEY

Hans My Hedgehog

•

He learns early on
there's something wrong with him—
his bed a pile of straw
hidden, flammable behind the stove,
a bowl of scraps on the floor.

His legs grow long
and his father's face
brightens at last, the old man
giving him the rooster,
the pigs, anything he wants,

giving him permission
to leave home.

•

Above the human feet
and the muscles of his legs,
above the tender genitalia
surrounded by curls, and the belly
with its shallow pit of navel

the quills begin—
sprouting through the flesh, foresting
back and shoulders, ending in a cap
just above the pointed snout:

Hans the bridegroom.

The princess who keeps her promises
shivers in her nightdress.
In the bridal chamber, candle-lit,
his quills seem to tremble
in the flickering shadows.

And before he lifts the linen sheet
and swings his legs into the bed,
before he holds her length against him

he strips off his pelt
as easily as clothing, drops it
like an empty mask—

the skin beneath in human form
burned black to the waist,
ready to be healed.

GWEN STRAUS

Cinderella

My step-sisters are willing
to cut off their toes for him.

What would I do for those days
when I played alone
in the hazel tree over my mother's grave?

I would go backwards if I could
and stay in that moment when the doves
fluttered down with the golden gown.

But everything has changed.
I trace his form in the ashes,
and then sweep it away before they see.

He's been on parade with that shoe.
All Prince, with heralds and entourage,
they come trumpeting through the village.

If he found me, would he recognize me,
my face, after mistaking their feet for mine?
I want to crawl away

into my pigeon house, my pear tree.
The world is too large, bright like a ballroom
and then suddenly dark.

Mother, no one prepared me for this—
for the soft heat of a man's neck when he dances
or the thickness of his arms.

MARGARET ATWOOD

The Robber Bridegroom

He would like not to kill. He would like
what he imagines other men have,
instead of this red compulsion. Why do the women
fail him and die badly? He would like to kill them gently,
finger by finger and with great tenderness, so that
at the end they would melt into him
with gratitude for his skill and the final pleasure
he still believes he could bring them
if only they would accept him,
but they scream too much and make him angry.
Then he goes for the soul, rummaging
in their flesh for it, despotic with self-pity,
hunting among the nerves and the shards
of their faces for the one thing
he needs to live, and lost
back there in the poplar and spruce forest
in the watery moonlight, where his young bride,
pale but only a little frightened,
her hands glimmering with his own approaching
death, gropes her way towards him
along the obscure path, from white stone
to white stone, ignorant and singing,
dreaming of him as he is.

MAURA STANTON

The Goosegirl

Imagine these geese—
how lice rave in the hulls of their feathers
infecting even you, your golden hair
tied up with black bootstring.
Under your fingernails, lice nibble.
Aren't you ashamed of those ruddy welts
crossing your neck?
When the prince arrives, hide in a thicket.
He will hunt your geese, calling: "Crows! White Crows!
All good fortune!"

Rumors of golden eggs
crop up in market gossip—
Should you flee the kingdom,
luring your geese with breadcrumbs?
The prince gallops in pursuit,
promising keepsakes, gilt brushes & bathtubs,
even a flock of swans!
All he wants: that swarm of dirty poultry
sniveling around your ankles.
"Lady! Please!" He offers half-a-kingdom.
You say, "And my hair?
Do you love my golden hair?"
He nods, disemboweling a goose
before your wrenched eyes with a pocketknife.

BRENDA HILLMAN

Rapunzel

A woman leans out of the window
And calls to the man
In the garden. His hands rest
On the shovel; her hair
Drips down the white wall.

He would climb up to her
If he wanted that artifice
But he has work to do, the important
Sun at his back.

The witch has kept them like this
For years. They have kept
The witch. She is what
We keep beyond all wisdom.
The witch is
Wanting too much.

Look at them
Posing, stunned and unaware:
One has the idea of labor,
One has the useless hair.

INGRID WENDT

The Fisherman's Wife

You know my story: the flounder my husband
caught, buying his freedom with magic.
Neat trick! True, I'd always wanted
a newer cottage, who among us doesn't
like an easier life? And I was ecstatic,
really, until my husband sauntered

in, smug, and demanded a kiss. More,
if the worst be told. As though
like the flounder, my freedom could be
had at a price; that I should adore
material things so much I'd show
my thanks between my grateful knees.

No matter if the heart was in it.
So why not ask for a bigger house?
A mansion? Palace? Kingdom? I
got everything, knowing of course this
is not what we live for. And of course
I knew I couldn't be God. But try

as I would, until that point no one
would challenge me, no one saw
anything wrong in asking for more than
I needed, in fact they urged me on.
What's protest without an audience?
Why not end it, be truly alone?

Last week, walking the beach I found
a glass fishing float. Seven
years it took to travel from Japan.
Fierce, the storm that ripped it out
of the parallel current, sent it
to lie robin's-egg fragile on sand.

Seven years ago I never
had heard of a flounder. Three
fisherman lost last week in the storm

were at home in all kinds of weather.
Three wives never could have dreamed of me,
jealous, with no clear right to mourn.

WANDA COLEMAN

Sex and Politics in Fairyland

rose red from across the tracks does
grow up to be a knockout. bold with big legs
and all the rest of the equipment necessary
to excite a prince

and if she plays her pumpkins right (she will)
she'll become snow white will acquire
all the material things wished upon

the big fine castle. servants of a darker race
the stretch limo. jewels and furs
champagne for a frivolous breakfast of
scrambled eggs and caviar

a smart dame from across the tracks, rose
has an instinct for opportunity—the savvy it
takes to get over. she knows she's got to score
before she's knocked up, starts to pudge out, or
otherwise loses her looks

this may require compromise—dyeing her hair
henna or ash, special hormones or cosmetic surgeries
and pretending a certain amount of ignorance
about the workings of fairytales

there will be critical moments when one word from
rose would change the story's plot. but she knows
her role and will hold her tongue. history
is the thorny realm of rich powerful princes

in the meantime rose can play games with trolls and
witches. her prince will tolerate it as long as
she doesn't cross him. as long as her game
doesn't interfere with his

and if she wants she can even make a sport of
equal height between normals & dwarfs. he will
understand. she needs to do something for
amusement—as long as the dwarfs
remain dwarfs

he will even allow her a wolf or two

thus our gal rose needn't concern herself
with the eternal sleep threatening the kingdom
she is assured resurrection by the local
sorcerer who offers happy endings
at a discount

ALIKI BARNSTONE

Fairy Tale

Before the good prince takes the good maid away
the fairy casts a spell on the evil sisters.

Each time they speak, lizards and snakes and toads
fall hissing from their mouths, as if the body

held in all bad and all the bad were released
embodied. Now since we're undressed for love

and love's a hard word, a lump in our throats,
a woman appears casting spells with her hands.

Her touch is awful, hurts, is good. Something
unspeakable she forces from our bodies.

It's worse than dirty. Not urine or feces
or what we know of sickness and of health.

It must be venom in all its consistencies,
the human secretions of anger, turning toward

and away, touch withheld, resentment, the child
happy and unafraid then ashamed and sulking.

Afterward you'd think we'd be cleansed. We have
a moment of quiet, hope, a kiss. But before

we're good again, I must be like the girl
who knit the sweater of nettles and then wore it,

who sucked three iron loaves down to nothing
while walking barefoot through desert and winter.

I'll live in three houses, and love and lose
each one. I must have three hateful husbands:

one who bores me, one who won't let me out
of his sight, one who beats me. Then I'll be free

to kiss you again. Then I'll wake from this dream
just as I did this morning. Spring light warmed

the sheets, my skin—so I wanted to make love
in the sun. But you would not hear my words

or feel my touch. I saw my evil sisters—
and all around me, hateful slithering things.

OLGA BROUMAS

Rapunzel

> *A woman*
> *who loves a woman*
> *is forever young.*
> Anne Sexton

Climb
through my hair, climb in
to me, love

hovers here like a mother's wish.
You might have been, though you're not
my mother.   You let loose like hair, like static
her stilled wish, relentless
in me and constant as
tropical growth.   Every hair

on my skin curled up, my spine
an enraptured circuit, a loop of memory, your first
private touch.   How many women
have yearned
for our lush perennial, found

themselves pregnant, and had
to subdue their heat, drown out their appetite
with pickles and harsh weeds.   How many
grew to confuse greed
with hunger, learned to grow thin on the bitter
root, the mandrake, on their sills.   *Old*

bitch, young
darling.   May those who speak them
choke on their words, their hunger freeze
in their veins like lard.
Less innocent

in my public youth
than you, less forbearing, I'll break the hush
of our cloistered garden, our harvest continuous
as a moan, the tilled bed luminous

with the future
yield. Red

vows like tulips.   Rows
upon rows of kisses from all lips.

ESSEX HEMPHILL

Song for Rapunzel

His hair
almost touches
his shoulders.
He dreams
of long braids,
ladders,
vines of hair.
He stands
like Rapunzel,
waiting on his balcony
to be rescued
from the fire-breathing
dragons of loneliness.
They breathe
at his hips
and thighs
the years soften
as they turn.
How long must he dream
ladders no one climbs?
He stands like Rapunzel,
growing deaf,
waiting
for a call.

7

THE GRIMM
SISTERHOOD

Her sisters in perfect focus.
MARTHA CARLSON-BRADLEY

I am a woman in a state of siege, alone
OLGA BROUMAS

For don't true sisters share?
EMMA BULL

INGRID WENDT

Cinderella Dream at Ten

Each night under the tree the same wolf
waits for The Beauty to fall
down into the gravel circle the children
draw each day for marbles
          (gravel fine as salt: ground
            into your knees it has to
            work itself out)

Each night the same wolf waits and no one
else is there to save
The Beauty waiting alone inside her

flowing yellow hair, the wolf snapping at her
plain blue skirts draped gracefully
over the lowest branch
          (skirts the mice her only real
            friends will trim with ribbons, lace, scraps
            her wicked stepsisters don't need)

So there's no question: each night
you in your father's car
          (your father driving)

drive past the playground, your heart
in your knees even before
you see her
          (in the tree where she always is)

struggle open the door,
struggle her into the seat beside you,
struggle to slam the door on the wolf who is
already gobbling down
          (as you knew he would, painlessly)

your own legs
from toes to knees

waking you
right at the hemline of your own short skirt

knowing it's happened before, your toes are
still there, not to cry out, knowing it's after

all the price you pay for Beauty.

ENID DAME

Cinderella

Every daughter has two mothers:
my good mother believes in government.
She loves and distrusts her house.
She scours the ceiling, scrubs the floor with a toothbrush.
Father's been gone for years.

My bad mother is an anarchist.
She sleeps late in a cobweb bed.
She walks through the house naked,
feeds tramps at the back door.

My good mother says, "Your body is disgusting.
It flops and bulges; it has no self-control.
I must keep you locked in this basement
because your smell would overpower the city.
Boys would fall out windows for lust of you.
A young woman is a walking swamp.
She leaks and oozes. Insects and toads cling to her hair.
She draws trouble
like a pile of manure draws flies."

My bad mother likes to walk barefoot
in mud. Cats and dogs sniff her crotch.
She laughs. She gathers flowers:
shameless daylilies,
demure black-eyed Susans,
bluebells seductively
open their skirts for her.
My bad mother says, "Trust your body."

My good mother gives me a necklace of cowrie shells.
I think they are ugly. They look like vaginas
with jagged, sharp teeth.
My bad mother hands me
a garland of dark red roses.
They are beautiful. But they too look like vaginas.

My good mother says, "If I let you go to the ball,
don't come home with a man or a belly.
If you do, I'll kill myself."

My bad mother says,
"Someday you'll bring home a man.
I'll make him chicken soup.
I'll knit you an afghan
to warm yourself under.
If he says your body smells like fern and rain-worked earth,
if he says your juices taste like flowers   then
stick with him.
Whoever he is,
he'll be a prince."

ROBIN MORGAN

The Two Gretels

The two Gretels were exploring the forest.
Hansel was home,
sending up flares.

Sometimes one Gretel got afraid.
She said to the other Gretel,
"I think I'm afraid."
"Of course we are," Gretel replied.

Sometimes the other Gretel whispered
with a shiver,
"You think we should turn back?"
To which her sister Gretel answered,
"We can't. We forgot the breadcrumbs."

So, they went forward
because
they simply couldn't imagine the way back.

And eventually, they found the Gingerbread House,
and the Witch, who was really, they discovered,
the Great Good Mother Goddess,
and they all lived happily ever after.

The Moral of this story is:

Those who would have the whole loaf,
let alone the House,
had better throw away their breadcrumbs.

MARTHA CARLSON-BRADLEY

One-Eye, Two-Eyes, Three-Eyes

The pretty one passes with ease
through crowded streets.

Stuffed with normalcy, she lives

on what her sisters leave behind:
crust and peelings, dirty spoons.

❖

Defined by an eye
in the middle of the forehead,

defined by three eyes,
set like a triangle in the skull,

they fall for her trick—a lullaby
sung to lashes, sung to lids:

are you open? are you closed?

❖

The knight carts her off,
fills her with love and food and wealth,
a tree of silver leaves and golden fruit
her wedding gift—

❖

Sister of excess. Sister of deficiency.

One-Eye, Three-Eyes at the door,
their clothes in rags,

One-Eye, Three-Eyes at the door,
their faces sunk down to the bone,

the lady of the castle
shares with them these rings of blue,

identical around each pupil—
that hole in the center

that restricts the light.
And lets it in.

Her sisters in perfect focus.

She offers them soup
and clean beds, a home,

returns kindness to those who were cruel:

the ugly ones, who set in motion
the magic that blessed her.

TERRI WINDLING

Brother and Sister

do you remember, brother
those days in the wood
when you ran with the deer
falling bloody on my doorstep at dusk
stepping from the skin
grateful to be a man
and do you know, brother
just how I longed
to wrap myself in the golden hide
smelling of musk
blackberries and rain
tell me *that* tale
give me *that* choice
and I'll choose speed and horn and hoof
give me that choice
all you cruel, clever fairies
and I'll choose the wood
not the prince

OLGA BROUMAS

Cinderella

> . . . the joy that isn't shared
> I heard, dies young.
> Anne Sexton, 1928-1974

Apart from my sisters, estranged
from my mother, I am a woman alone
in a house of men
who secretly
call themselves princes, alone
with me usually, under cover of dark.   I am the one allowed in

to the royal chambers, whose small foot conveniently
fills the slipper of glass.   The woman writer, the lady
umpire, the madam chairman, anyone's wife.
I know what I know.
And I once was glad

of the chance to use it, even alone
in a strange castle, doing overtime on my own, cracking
the royal code.   The princes spoke
in their fathers' language, were eager to praise me
my nimble tongue.   I am a woman in a state of siege, alone

as one piece of laundry, strung on a windy clothesline a
mile long. A woman co-opted by promises: the lure
of a job, the ruse of a choice, a woman forced
to bear witness, falsely
against my kind, as each
other sister was judged inadequate, bitchy, incompetent,
jealous, too thin, too fat.   I know what I know.
What sweet bread I make

for myself in this prosperous house
is dirty, what good soup I boil turns
in my mouth to mud.   Give
me my ashes.   A cold stove, a cinder-block pillow, wet
canvas shoes in my sisters', my sisters' hut.   Or I swear

I'll die young
like those favored before me, hand-picked each one
for her joyful heart.

ANDREA HOLLANDER BUDY

Gretel

A woman is born to this:
sift, measure, mix, roll thin.

She learns the dough until
it folds into her skin and there is

no difference. Much later
she tries to lose it. Makes bets

with herself and wins enough
to keep trying. One day she begins

that long walk in unfamiliar woods.
She means to lose everything

she is. She empties her dark pockets,
dropping enough crumbs

to feed all the men who have ever
touched her or wished.

When she reaches the clearing
she is almost transparent—

so thin
the old woman in the house seizes

only the brother. You know the rest:
She won't escape that oven. She'll eat

the crumbs meant for him, remember
something of his touch, reach

for the sifter and the cup.

JANE YOLEN

Fat Is Not a Fairy Tale

I am thinking of a fairy tale,
Cinder Elephant,
Sleeping Tubby,
Snow Weight,
where the princess is not
anorexic, wasp-waisted,
flinging herself down the stairs.

I am thinking of a fairy tale,
Hansel and Great,
Repoundsel,
Bounty and the Beast,
where the beauty
has a pillowed breast,
and fingers plump as sausage.

I am thinking of a fairy tale
that is not yet written,
for a teller not yet born,
for a listener not yet conceived,
for a world not yet won,
where everything round is good:
the sun, wheels, cookies, and the princess.

ERIN BELIEU

Rose Red

She never wanted the troll,

though, when freeing his beard
trapped in the bill of a circling bird,
when sliding her scissors through the soft
hairs at the nub of his chin, she did
think the shadow dropping from the gull's
wings lent his face a certain ugly interest.

She never wanted the prince's brother,

second prize to the elder, but just as vain,
with a woman's soft hips and hands,
surrounding himself with mirrors and liking
her sister better anyway, her indiscriminate
sweetness: an ordinary fruit ripening
in a bowl displayed on a public table.

And she did not want the bear

their mother invited next to the fire,
though his stinking fur could make
her eyes and mouth water. Once, she devised
a way to lie beside him, innocently
at first, then not so, curled behind him,
running her thumbnail down his spine.

What she wanted, of course, was her own place in the forest,

where she would take the flowering trees
that grew outside her mother's bedroom window—
one white, buxom with albino blossoms,
one red, smaller, with delicate, hooked thorns—
and plant them on opposite sides of her cottage,
watching each bloom fall as summer spoiled them.

EMMA BULL

The Stepsister's Story

I knew you, dancing.
She said, "Who is that?"
The others said it, too.
But I knew.

I thought the word she would not let me say.
Sister. You danced by so close
I could have touched the tiny buttons down your back.
I kept your secret, as true sisters do.

You were not more beautiful
Spinning in a cloud of silk,
Laughing in spangle-light,
Than on that cold hearth.

Not more beautiful
Than when my eyes crept secretly toward you
To the line of your bent white neck
And I thought, Sister.

Not more beautiful
Than your fair closed ash-marked face.
Ash-bruised fingers took the poker, made the fire dance
And I thought, I love you.

Who closed the tiny buttons down your back?
I would have done that sister's work.
You would have made the boys who loved you
Dance with me first.

Oh, tomorrow, don't let her see
That fallen sequin, that unguarded smile.
She'll be wild to think that you were happy.
Never be happy out loud
And I'll keep the secret.

The shoe came.
She locked you in the pantry.
She brought it to me, still full of spangle-light
And the chime of your laugh.

I did it to share your laugh and the cloud of silk
For don't true sisters share?
I did it to dance away from fear, from her,
To dance you away in my arms and call you sister.
True sisters ride to rescue, and I would
If only the shoe fit.

We'll make it fit, she said.
The kitchen knife was not full of spangle-light
And this is not how I meant to share with you.

Light-headed, I rode away,
My arms around the prince's waist,
Blood welling from your shoe
To stain the white horse flank.

And as the spangles danced before my eyes
I thought I might be you, riding safely away,
That I was the one she'd shut in darkness,
That we'd both slipped from her grasp at last.

I can't dance now.
But I would sit on your hearth
And stir the fire to dancing with a crutch.
Let me sit near your happiness.
Let me warm myself at your laughter.
Let me say at last, where she can't hear,
Sister, sister, sister.

MARGARET ATWOOD

Girl Without Hands

Walking through the ruins
on your way to work
that do not look like ruins
with the sunlight pouring over
the seen world
like hail or melted
silver, that bright
and magnificent, each leaf
and stone quickened and specific in it,
and you can't hold it,
you can't hold any of it. Distance surrounds you,
marked out by the ends of your arms
when they are stretched to their fullest.
You can go no farther than this,
you think, walking forward,
pushing the distance in front of you
like a metal cart on wheels
with its barriers and horizontals.
Appearance melts away from you,
the offices and pyramids
on the horizon shimmer and cease.
No one can enter that circle
you have made, that clean circle
of dead space you have made
and stay inside,
mourning because it is clean.

Then there's the girl, in the white dress,
meaning purity, or the failure
to be any colour. She has no hands, it's true.
The scream that happened to the air
when they were taken off
surrounds her now like an aureole
of hot sand, of no sound.
Everything has bled out of her.

Only a girl like this
can know what's happened to you.
If she were here she would
reach out her arms towards
you now, and touch you
with her absent hands
and you would feel nothing, but you would be
touched all the same.

NICOLE COOLEY

Rampion

Tiny blue flowers furred with dirt are all the woman desires
in the story my mother reads over and over. Once upon a time

a woman longed for a child, but see how one desire easily
replaces the next, see her husband climbing the high garden wall

with a handful of rampion, flowering scab she's traded for a child.
Look, my mother says, see how the mother disappears

as rampion's metallic root splits the tongue like a knife
and the daughter spends the rest of the story alone.

I study a watercolor of the daughter's tower where she waits
for the prince, twisting and spinning her long shining hair. Already

I know I will grow up to be that bad mother, throat stuffed with dust,
mouth a blistering ache, promising anything, forgetting

the baby swimming inside me, baby the size of a fist, baby
taking root. This is the lesson: the mother drops out of the story.

See, my mother reads, *the woman pines away with desire*
but understand it's the wrong, selfish kind

because the mother's body should be just a country
the girl departs—pure blank horizon.

ANNIE FINCH

To the Nixie of the Mill-Pond

Nixie, I will comb
my hair down through the water
till it reaches your home.
I will be your daughter.

I know my husband's life
was covered with this fear.
Now he rises alive
out of your swimming air,

and I am freed, with gold
and dreams and a crone's advice,
to reach with my womanhood
through the surface of your life.

What do you want from me?
Why do I need to comb
and play the flute and spin
at the edge of your ancient home?

I am alive for him,
and he is my rescued love.
I offer my golden skills
for you to weave power of:

power of my black hair,
power of my golden voice,
power of the endless thread
to weave your commingling trace;

Nixie, I will send
a song down through the water
till it reaches your home.
I will be your daughter.

I will not be the same;
I will turn hard like a toad;
I will only be his wife again
at the end of a hard, equal road.

Nixie, I will spin
my flax down through the water
till it reaches your home.
I will be your daughter.

OLGA BROUMAS

Little Red Riding Hood

I grow old, old
without you, Mother, landscape
of my heart.   No child, no daughter between my bones
has moved, and passed
out screaming, dressed in her mantle of blood

as I did
once through your pelvic scaffold, stretching it
like a wishbone, your tenderest skin
strung on its bow and tightened
against the pain.   I slipped out like an arrow, but not before

the midwife
plunged to her wrist and guided
my baffled head to its first mark.   High forceps
might, in that one instant, have accomplished
what you and that good woman failed
in all these years to do: cramp
me between the temples, hobble
my baby feet.   Dressed in my red hood, howling, I went—

evading
the white-clad doctor and his fancy claims: microscope,
stethoscope, scalpel, all
the better to see with, to hear,
and to eat—straight from your hollowed basket
into the midwife's skirts.   I grew up

good at evading, and when you said,
"Stick to the road and forget the flowers, there's
wolves in those bushes, mind
where you got to go, mind
you get there," I
minded.   I kept

to the road, kept
the hood secret, kept what it sheathed more
secret still. I opened
it only at night, and with other women
who might be walking the same road to their own
grandma's house, each with her basket of gifts, her small hood
safe in the same part. I minded well. I have no daughter

to trace that road, back to your lap with my laden
basket of love. I'm growing
old, old
without you. Mother, landscape
of my heart, architect of my body, what other gesture
can I conceive

to make with it
that would reach you, alone
in your house and waiting, across this improbable forest
peopled with wolves and our lost, flower-gathering
sisters they feed on.

THYLIAS MOSS

Lessons from a Mirror

Snow White was nude at her wedding, she's so white
the gown seemed to disappear when she put it on.

Put me beside her and the proximity is good
for a study of chiaroscuro, not much else.

Her name aggravates me most, as if I need to be told
what's white and what isn't.

Judging strictly by appearance there's a future for me
forever at her heels, a shadow's constant worship.

Is it fair for me to live that way, unable
to get off the ground?

Turning the tables isn't fair unless they keep turning.
Then there's the danger of Russian roulette

and my disadvantage: nothing falls from the sky
to name me.

I am the empty space where the tooth was, that my tongue
rushes to fill because I can't stand vacancies.

And it's not enough. The penis just fills another
gap. And it's not enough.

When you look at me,
know that more than white is missing.

CAROL JANE BANGS

The Wicked Witch

. . . to the wise
Often, often is it denied
To be beautiful or good.
W. H. Auden, "Oxford"

She greets her mirror, eager as a child;
Eighty years pull back to the bone,
the skin drawn thin as paper
over cheek and skull.
Lips part over yellow teeth
ground half down to the gum.
Nostrils open on a black vault.
Thin hair frizzles from her scarf
like a halo of white frost.

And the eyes peer over ravaged lids
like the eyes of a newborn child,
who, having seen all that is,
has everything to forget.
Age draws her closer to the awareness
that the appearance of goodness
is all that we know of the Good.
What use has an old woman for propriety,
her body having failed to give her pleasure,
beauty neither a thing of the past
nor a trusted potential.
She sees in the mirror no more, no less
than what has lived there forever.

History treats her badly, this crone.
She never had victims; they had themselves,
falling under the spell of their own beauty,
stumbling through their own dark forests,
unprepared, no lamp in hand.
The poison apple dropped
from Snow White's own tree.
Hansel's cage grew out of his bones.
Rapunzel's tower was coiled from her plaits

and the Frog Prince fathered no heirs.
Who's to tell what Sleeping Beauty dreamed
before waking to marriage and decorum,
the ennui of ever-after?

These crooked hands could be murderers.
The thin lips could move to deceive.
Lacking goodness or beauty the old woman
knows the roots of the oldest tales.
For a witch knows the world the way it is,
looks into the mirror long past the age
when a princess would look away.

JULIA ALVAREZ

Against Cinderella

Whoever made it up is pulling my foot
so it'll fit that shoe.
I'll go along with martyrdom—
she swept and wept, mended, stoked the fire,
slaved while her three stepsisters,
who just happened to oblige their meanness
by being ugly, dressed themselves.
I'll swallow that there was a Singer godmother
who magically could sew a pattern up
and hem it in an hour,
that Cinderella got to be a debutante
and lost her head and later lost her shoe.
But there I stop.
I can't believe only one woman in that town
had that size foot, could fit into that shoe.
I've felt enough of lost and found
to know that if you lose your heart
to anyone you've crowned into a prince,
you might not get it back.
That the old kerchief trick,
whether you drop a shoe, your clothes, your life,
doesn't do much but litter up the world.
That when the knock at last comes to your door,
you might not be home or willing.
That some of us have learned to go barefoot
knowing the mate to one foot is the other.

8 VARIATIONS & UPDATES

*You can see such a long way
into the story.*

ALICE WIRTH GRAY

I dress in the latest Paris originals

DAVID TRINIDAD

*up pops this frog
musta come from the sewer*

KATHARYN HOWD MACHAN

RANDALL JARRELL

The Sleeping Beauty: Variation of the Prince

After the thorns I came to the first page.
He lay there gray in his fur of dust:
As I bent to open an eye, I sneezed.
But the ball looked by me, blue
As the sky it stared into . . .
And the sentry's cuirass is red with rust.

Children play inside: the dirty hand
Of the little mother, an inch from the child
That has worn out, burst, and blown away,
Uncurling to it—does not uncurl.
The bloom on the nap of their world
Is set with thousands of dawns of dew.

But at last, at the center of all the webs
Of the realm established in your blood,
I find you; and—look!—the drop of blood
Is there still, under the dust of your finger:
I force it, slowly, down from your finger
And it falls and rolls away, as it should.

And I bend to touch (just under the dust
That was roses once) the steady lips
Parted between a breath and a breath
In love, for the kiss of the hunter, Death.
Then I stretch myself beside you, lay
Between us, there in the dust, His sword.

When the world ends—it will never end—
The dust at last will fall from your eyes
In judgment, and I shall whisper:
"For hundreds of thousands of years I have slept
Beside you, here in the last long world
That you had found; that I have kept."

When they come for us—no one will ever come—
I shall stir from my long light sleep,
I shall whisper, "Wait, wait! . . . She is asleep."
I shall whisper, gazing, up to the gaze of the hunter,
Death, and close with the tips of the dust of my hand
The lids of the steady—

                            Look, He is fast asleep!

BRUCE BENNETT

The True Story of Snow White

Almost before the princess had grown cold
Upon the floor beside the bitten fruit,
The Queen gave orders to her men to shoot
The dwarfs, and thereby clinched her iron hold
Upon the state. Her mirror learned to lie,
And no one dared speak ill of her for fear
She might through her devices overhear.
So, in this manner, many years passed by,
And now today not even children weep
When someone whispers how, for her beauty's sake,
A child was harried once into a grove
And doomed, because her heart was full of love,
To lie forever in unlovely sleep
Which not a prince on earth has power to break.

MIKE CARLIN

Anaconda Mining Makes the Seven Dwarfs an Offer

Fifty-million to buy them out
including mineral rights.
Only Happy isn't smiling

knowing how lost they'd be
in a Brentwood townhouse
and not one of them equipped

to take on muggers, capital gains shelters,
Assembly of God proselytizers, dioxin
in the fish. Imagine the trauma

their air sacs are in for, sopping up the smog.
Even in the country, where could they find
another valley as enchanted

or unlogged? As free
from KKK friendship cook-outs
and jet-fighter training flights?

Of course, black lung
might already be whistling
while they work.

RACHEL LODEN

HM Customs & Excise

The disposal of the remains of the dead is exempt from VAT.

Six mice built a little carriage to carry her to her grave, and when the carriage was ready they harnessed themselves to it, and the cock drove.

In practice this means that: your provision of the services of embalming and the digging and preparation and refilling of graves is always tax-exempt.

Hearse-light. *Hearse*, a buriall carriage couered with blacke—

Above it, a small box of light wood: it is the coffin of a child, covered with wildflowers.

Your supply of bell-tolling is also exempt.

As for the articles placed in the coffin, the hats have bands but no strings to tie them to the head.

Then the little cock was left alone with the dead hen, and dug a grave for her and laid her in it, and made a mound above it, on which he sat down and fretted until he died too, and then everyone was dead.

A carriage is driven to the grave and buried there, but it has no bells or reins attached.

SARA HENDERSON HAY

Juvenile Court

Deep in the oven, where the two had shoved her,
They found the Witch, burned to a crisp, of course.
And when the police had decently removed her,
They questioned the children, who showed no remorse.
"She threatened us," said Hansel, "with a kettle
Of boiling water, just because I threw
The cat into the well." Cried little Gretel,
"She fussed because I broke her broom in two,

And said she'd lock up Hansel in a cage
For drawing funny pictures on her fence . . ."
Wherefore the court, considering their age,
And ruling that there seemed some evidence
The pair had acted under provocation,
Released them to their parents, on probation.

ENID DAME

The Social Worker Finds
Hansel and Gretel Difficult to Place

Why can't I find a home
for these *schöne kinder?*
This good boy
spent most of his life in a cage
isolated from evil.
This clever girl
reduced their captor to rubbish.
These children instinctively
knew how to seize the moment,
to strike hard and thrust the blow home.
Mothers of Germany,
why won't you carry these darlings
back to your well-stocked kitchens?
Why do you only stare
into their cool blue eyes,
then turn away?

ALICE WIRTH GRAY

On a Nineteenth Century Color Lithograph
of Red Riding Hood by the Artist J. H.

The wolf makes a funny face
not to be taken seriously as evil,
but as if there's something wrong
with his eyes. He's old
and getting cataracts or he's
trying to start a conversation
by winking at Riding Hood,
where she stands by a cheery spread
of amanita phalloides, wondering
how to get back to her basket of goodies
which she left on the other side
of the clearing while gathering flowers,
and now of course the wolf blocks her way.
Some people have a crucifix over the bed:
I have a wolf.

The NIGHT POLICE Interrogate Riding Hood:
Nice try, kid, but daisies don't grow
in that woods. Look at those trees,
their trunks acid-green with moss.
There's not enough light in there
for an impatiens or cineraria.
And that basket with the bottle
of Bordeaux sticking out. Explain that.
This is a German forest if ever one was:
grim Grimm, blacker than Black.
Don't you tell us about Perrault:
for you all stories with fear in them
will always be German. Your mom
is sending you through these woods
by yourself with a bottle of imported wine?
You expect us to buy that?
Save us all time.
You knew that wolf.
You've been encouraging him.

I've always loved that picture
because there's Riding Hood far left
and the wolf far right
and the center absolutely empty.
So much space between girl and wolf
that is so much more interesting
than either of them. You can see
into and into the woods
until it's so dark you can't.
You can see such a long way
into the story.

What RIDING HOOD Told the Cops:
Of course I talked to him,
it's what the books say to do:
try to keep them talking.
Reason with them. Look, Mr. Wolf,
sit down. We'll drink this bottle.
Then we'll go on to Grandma's
and redden our teeth on her.
They sent me here.
They must have known
the way the world is.

Myself, I would like to get past
all that little-girl-and-the-wolf thing
into the dark beyond them both.

Honestly, I thought it must be
a rite of passage. That the solution
might be hidden in the basket
under the white cloth.
When I peeked, I found
she'd sent me off in the dark
without so much as a flashlight.

The Report of the NIGHT POLICE continues:
We picked the girl up in the woods.
Rather, what we mean to say is
that's where we took her into custody.
She looks like an angel,
but you just can't tell.

What was in the basket,
we wanted to know. Was she
trying to get rid of something?
We asked her to explain herself,
and she says her mother
hung the lithograph of a wolf
over her bed. A likely story.
What woman would do a thing like that?
There may be enough evidence
to run her folks in, too.

The WOLF:
For God's sake.
I was lost.
Can't you tell?
She seemed to mistake me
for someone she knew.
I didn't want to frighten her.
You're not going to try
to hang this one on me,
are you? I'd never
have gone there alone.
That's why we always
travel in packs.
I mean it's dark in there.
Dangerous.

Testimony of the HUNTER:
So I heard all this yelling
from the old lady's cottage
a female in distress I sez
and I don't think twice
but bust down the door
gun at the ready
and that kid and the wolf
(that's him over there,
yer honor) well, you wouldn't
believe it, the amount of blood
and that kid does she have
a mouth on her it embarrasses me
when girls talk so foul like that
if she was my daughter

I'd beat her till she was civil
and I'd crack all the teeth
in her dirty mouth and I'd
take away her clothes and lock her up
to sit in her own filth until
she'd learned a little respect.
What's that, sir? You want me
to stand down? Well, sure,
if you say so.

MOTHER:
Of course I hung the lithograph
over her bed. It's a work of art.
You think something like that
is going to scare that child?
Anyway, I had to put it somewhere,
it was a gift. And let me tell you,
there was a perfectly safe path
around those woods,
through a public park,
and well patrolled.
But not her.
You couldn't keep her
from looking for trouble,
and able to find it
where there is none.
My husband was no help at all:
what do you expect a mother to do?
Oh, if only
we'd been rich enough
to buy her a car.

It was all so complicated:
who was this Riding Hood?
I never liked the grandmother.
Sometimes the wolf wasn't so bad:
he could have eaten the girl
there in the forest but he
put off a present treat
to eat a stringy old lady
in the future. That's not
the reasoning of a beast.

Then, never did I doubt
he liked Riding Hood
more than the others did.
What do you mean?
What do I see in the picture?
Is this some kind of Rorschach?
I want to talk to my attorney.
It was my mother
who hung the picture
over my bed.
Those dark woods,
beckoning,
a challenge.
A place to go to
from the place you are.

DAVID TRINIDAD

The Peasant Girl

Sometimes it is to one's advantage to do good deeds.
I know this from personal experience. You see,
one afternoon my abrasive stepmother sent me
to the spring well over a mile from our cottage
to fetch water for her daily bath. As usual, I
passed through the village in my tattered dress, daydreaming,
swinging the empty pail, alternating it from hand
to hand. At the spring, I sat on a fresh patch of grass
and rested, leaning over and gazing at my face
on the smooth surface of the water. Coal smeared my cheeks.
Suddenly, a warped form disrupted my reflection
like a thrown pebble or stone. It was a decrepit
woman who had appeared out of nowhere, a real witch.
Her long nose protruded from beneath her loose black hood
like a half-nibbled cob of corn, her hands were withered
and spotted like old cabbage leaves, and her voice cracked like
the shells of walnuts when she uttered: "Would you be kind
enough to give a tired workingwoman a cool drink?"
What the heck, I thought, I've nothing better to do.
So I dipped the ladle into the spring and held it up
to her parched lips. But she was no longer
an old woman; that was only a disguise. She was
actually a good fairy: wand, glitter, gauzy wings
and all. And she spoke in a sweet unruffled voice:
"I shall reward you for your deed. Whenever you speak,
beautiful flowers and priceless gems shall flow
into the world with your words." I ran home in a stupor
of excitement, my unwashed hair flying behind me
like steam from a locomotive, and told my stepmother
about the fairy and how I had passed her silly
test, and as I spoke, a dozen rubies splattered
on the wooden floor like drops of blood. "Keep talking,"
said my stepmother. I did, and orchids tumbled from my mouth,
and gold coins, and pearl rings, and then white chrysanthemums,
irises, violets, sapphires, jonquils, carnations,
strings of sweet peas streaming as long as my sentences,
crystal goblets, asters, opals, pieces of topaz,

jade pears. Daisies popped into the air like periods,
and turquoise and gladiolas fell until a large pile
shone in front of us so brightly, it seemed
the sun had set in the middle of our living room.
Gaping, my stepmother bent down to stuff all
of the valuables into her apron pockets. When
she looked up, a sudden admiration, like emeralds,
glistened in her eyes. Now a local girl fetches our water
from the distant spring. I'm served breakfast in bed.
I dress in the latest Paris originals and
visit the hairdresser. And whether I speak kindness,
insult, or untruth, the roses roll off my tongue
and diamonds sparkle as they drip from my gifted lips.

DENISE DUHAMEL

The Ugly Stepsister

You don't know what it was like.
My mother marries this bum who takes off on us,
after only a few months, leaving his little Cinderella
behind. Oh yes, Cindy will try to tell you
that her father died. She's like that, she's a martyr.
But between you and me, he took up
with a dame close to Cindy's age.
My mother never got a cent out of him
for child support. So that explains
why sometimes the old lady was gruff.
My sisters and I didn't mind Cindy at first,
but her relentless cheeriness soon took its toll.
She dragged the dirty clothes to one of Chelsea's
many laundromats. She was fond of talking
to mice and rats on the way. She loved doing dishes
and scrubbing walls, taking phone messages,
and cleaning toilet bowls. You know,
the kind of woman that makes the rest
of us look bad. My sisters and I
weren't paranoid, but we couldn't help
but see this manic love for housework
as part of Cindy's sinister plan. Our dates
would come to pick us up and Cindy'd pop out
of the kitchen offering warm chocolate chip cookies.
Critics often point to the fact that my sisters and I
were dark and she was blonde, implying
jealousy on our part. But let me
set the record straight. We have the empty bottles
of Clairol's Nice 'n Easy to prove
Cindy was a fake. She was what her shrink called
a master manipulator. She loved people
to feel bad for her—her favorite phrase was a faint,
"I don't mind. That's OK." We should have known
she'd marry Jeff Charming, the guy from our high school
who went on to trade bonds. Cindy finagled her way
into a private Christmas party on Wall Street,
charging a little black dress at Barney's,

which she would have returned the next day
if Jeff hadn't fallen head over heels.
She claimed he took her on a horse-and-buggy ride
through Central Park, that it was the most romantic
evening of her life, even though she was home
before midnight—a bit early, if you ask me, for Manhattan.
It turned out that Jeff was seeing someone else
and had to cover his tracks. But Cindy didn't
let little things like another woman's happiness
get in her way. She filled her glass slipper
with champagne she had lifted
from the Wall Street extravaganza. She toasted
to Mr. Charming's coming around, which he did
soon enough. At the wedding, some of Cindy's friends
looked at my sisters and me with pity. The bride insisted
that our bridesmaids' dresses should be pumpkin,
which is a hard enough color for anyone to carry off.
But let me assure you, we're all very happy
now that Cindy's moved uptown. We've
started a mail order business—cosmetics
and perfumes. Just between you and me,
there's quite a few bucks to be made
on women's self-doubts. And though
we don't like to gloat, we hear Cindy Charming
isn't doing her aerobics anymore. It's rumored
that she yells at the maid, then locks herself in her room,
pressing hot match tips into her palm.

DOROTHY HEWETT

Grave Fairytale

I sat in my tower, the seasons whirled,
the sky changed, the river grew
and dwindled to a pool.
The black Witch, light as an eel,
laddered up my hair
to straddle the window-sill.

She was there when I woke, blocking the light,
or in the night, humming, trying on my clothes.
I grew accustomed to her; she was as much a part of me
as my own self; sometimes I thought, "She *is* myself!"
a posturing blackness, savage as a cuckoo.

There was no mirror in the tower.

Each time the voice screamed from the thorny garden
I'd rise and pensively undo the coil,
I felt it switch the ground, the earth tugged at it,
once it returned to me knotted with dead warm birds,
once wrapped itself three times around the tower—
                            the tower quaked.
Framed in the window, whirling the countryside
with my great net of hair I'd catch a hawk,
                            a bird, and once a bear.
One night I woke, the horse pawed at the walls,
the cell was full of light, all my stone house
suffused, the voice called from the calm white garden,
                            "Rapunzel."
I leant across the sill, my plait hissed out
                            and spun like hail;
he climbed, slow as a heartbeat, up the stony side,
we dropped together as he loosed my hair,
his foraging hands tore me from neck to heels:
the witch jumped up my back and beat me to the wall.

Crouched in a corner I perceived it all,
the thighs jack-knifed apart, the dangling sword
                            thrust home,

pinned like a specimen—to scream with joy.
I watched all night the beasts unsatisfied
roll in their sweat, their guttural cries
made the night thick with sound.
Their shadows gambolled, hunch-backed, hairy-arsed,
and as she ran four-pawed across the light,
the female dropped coined blood spots on the floor.

When morning came he put his armour on,
kissing farewell like angels swung on hair.
I heard the metal shoes trample the round earth
      about my tower.
Three times I lent my hair to the glowing prince,
hand over hand he climbed, my roots ached,
the blood dribbled on the stone sill.
Each time I saw the framed-faced bully boy
      sick with his triumph.

The third time I hid the shears,
a stab of black ice dripping in my dress.
He rose, his armour glistened in my tears,
the convex scissors snapped,
the glittering coil hissed, and slipped
      through air to undergrowth.
His mouth, like a round O, gaped at his end,
his finger nails ripped out, he clawed through space.
His horse ran off flank-deep in blown thistles.
Three seasons he stank at the tower's base.
A hawk plucked out his eyes, the ants busied his brain,
the mud-weed filled his mouth, his great sword rotted,
his tattered flesh-flags hung on bushes for the birds.

Bald as a collaborator I sit walled
      in the thumb-nosed tower,
wound round three times with ropes of autumn leaves.
And the witch…sometimes I idly kick
a little heap of rags across the floor.
I notice it grows smaller every year.

MARIA TERRONE

Rapunzel: A Modern Tale

She played rhythm and blues, hair
   'round her feet a hoop of fire
no one dared

come near. Village denizens
   adored her from afar,
whispering about childhood horrors:

that witch of a mother,
   years spent alone
locked in a room. Her song

was the rope she used to escape.
   It stretched miles across rivers,
reaching the Prince

of Kings Highway
   who resolved to find her,
to climb that high, sweet sound.

I'll free you, he called out,
   pushing through the tavern.
I am free, she said, and signaled

her Merlin. Floodlights poured.
   Blinded, the Prince tripped
on Rapunzel's hair, then spent

the next decade in grief
   and wandering until he fell again,
this time for a shaved-head beauty.

AMY GERSTLER

Scorched Cinderella

This sooty beauty can't yet shed light.
But soon she'll exude a myopic glow
even our cynical paperboy won't be immune to.
Her little hands are cold as Saturn.
She has the accusing eyes of some dying
feline. Her unfettered mind grinds like
a sawmill, or it tinkles like chandeliers
breezes are fingering. She ignites
n'er-do-wells and solid citizens
alike. She demanded we tattoo an axe
and a skull on her pelvic girdle:
guideposts for explorers hoping to plant
their flags in her lost continent.
Her hair's a forest of totem poles.
Her feet, scentless orchids, cherish
their seclusion in the twin greenhouses
of her heavy corrective shoes. She dines
on hawk wings, beets and unspeakable
custards. How can any of us, daughters
of our mother's disastrous first marriage,
hope to land husbands with her around?
We suffer by comparison with every tick
of the clock. Some say that next to her
we're like stray dogs who scavenge grass
all winter, or quick lizards skittering
along pantry shelves behind dusty pickle
jars. We've locked our sister up, covered
her with tiny cuts. She insists she likes
her hair better since we singed it.
She says people are whispering inside
the air conditioner. It's getting harder
to slap her awake every day to face
the purer girl we're scouring her down to,
but she's still worth a detour,
if you happen to be passing through.

RIGOBERTO GONZÁLEZ

The Girl With No Hands

Your father asked for more than a polka-dot tie, a self-portrait in
     Crayola or cinnamon
snickerdoodles flat as candle stubs on the baking sheet. He grabbed
     you by the wrists

and severed your hands to wear on his key chain like a pair of lucky
     rabbit's feet.
What is so fortunate about a rabbit hopping about the prairie with a
     missing limb?

What if all four of its legs had been clipped? It eats only as far as it can
     stretch
its neck, and then rolls itself on its back to perforate its starved belly
     with the blades

of its ribs. When the hunter returns, the rabbit will have its revenge,
     looking like
the amputated foot of his diabetic mother wearing that familiar bunny
     slipper.

Your father seized your hands, not out of malice, but greed—his wish
     to match
Midas and pocket the small golds of his kingdom—Rolex, wedding
     bands, crucifix,

and the precious treasures of your rings, which, little princess, will
     never leave
your fingers because Papi breaks no promises. He never abandoned
     you either,

always there when you come across your hairbrush, perched on the
     bristles
like a nesting pecker. Resolute, you age with ingenuity, learning to eat

right off the branch, nibbling apple, apricot and pear without
     separating fruit
from stem. This is how you heard about the clever rabbit, from the
     hunter's son

who made love to you pressing his fists to the small of his back. He locked you
against the tree trunk and your shoulders splintered the bark. What a miracle

of an instrument, the piano that's played with elbows and knees and four clumsy
heels that for all their random reaching make the sweetest rhythms. Your bodies

danced each afternoon in the grove while your mother sewed the mysterious
tears in your dresses. You forgave your mother's inactivity that night when Papi

struck down your wrists with a cleaver, the mirror of the metal like a window
to a furnace, the shadow puppet butterfly emancipated finally. Who knew

chopped bone could sing? Maybe chicken doesn't utter a note at its beheading
because its mother hen isn't near to cluck a frenzied requiem. Your mother

squealed as fiercely as a sow and your stumps looked like the bloodied snouts
of swine. But all that rage escapes you now as you unleash the power of the hand

your father left intact, and with it grip your lover tighter into you. So this
is delectable defiance, Miss Rabbit—it must have been a female to claim

the last word. You, girl with no hands, can produce another pair and more:
legs, torso, head, and a bear trap of a jaw to bite the hands that feed her.

R. S. GWYNN

Snow White and the Seven Deadly Sins

Good Catholic girl, she didn't mind the cleaning.
All of her household chores, at first, were small
And hardly labors one could find demeaning.
One's duty was one's refuge, after all.

And if she had her doubts at certain moments
And once confessed them to the Father, she
Was instantly referred to texts in Romans
And Peter's First Epistle, chapter III.

Years passed. More sinful every day, the *Seven*
Breakfasted, grabbed their pitchforks, donned their horns
And sped to contravene the hopes of heaven,
Sowing the neighbors' lawns with tares and thorns.

She set to work. *Pride's* hundred looking-glasses
Ogled her dimly, smeared with prints of lips;
Lust's magazines lay strewn—bare tits and asses
With flyers for new "devices"—chains, cuffs, whips.

Gluttony's empties covered half the table,
Mingling with *Avarice's* cards and chips,
And she'd been told to sew a Bill Blass label
In the green blazer *Envy'd* bought at Gyp's.

She knelt to the cold master bathroom floor as
If a petitioner before the Pope,
Retrieving several pairs of *Sloth's* soiled drawers,
A sweat-sock and a cake of hairy soap.

Then, as she wiped the Windex from the mirror,
She noticed, and the vision made her cry,
How much she'd grayed and paled, and how much clearer
Festered the bruise of *Wrath* beneath her eye.

"No poisoned apple needed for this Princess,"
She murmured, making X's with her thumb.
A car door slammed, bringing her to her senses:
Ho-hum. Ho-hum. It's home from work we come.

And she was out the window in a second,
In time to see a *Handsome Prince*, of course,
Who, spying her distressed condition, beckoned
For her to mount (What else?) his snow-white horse.

Impeccably he spoke. His smile was glowing.
So debonair! So charming! And so *Male*.
She took one step, reversed, and without slowing
Beat it to St. Anne's where she took the veil.

ALICE WIRTH GRAY

Snow White and the Man Sent to Fetch Her Heart

> *. . . she began to weep, and said: "Ah, dear huntsman,*
> *leave me my life! I will run away into the wild forest, and*
> *never come home again."*
>
> The Brothers Grimm

Think carefully. That's what
you said that did the trick?
It would be cruelty
to give us the wrong charm
when we get no second chance.
We know, of course, that you
were gorgeous. Was that all
it was, and you need not
have opened your mouth?

Perhaps he was a revolutionary,
set to do anything contrary
to the old Queen's interests.
Or else the death at his hands
each year of myriad stags, wolves
and quail quelled his bloodlust,
left him empty of hostility,
a peaceable kingdom all of himself.
His relationships with people
were impeccable. He worried
that abortion was really murder.

Perhaps he found you irresistible,
Snow White, and you promised him
something? And the whole
seamy story got suppressed
when your party came to power?
A nasty piece of business,
if you had the man done in
when he came for his pay-off;
or if you gave him what he wanted
and left us, poor suckers, thinking

it was all done with no *quid pro quo,*
turning the affair into something
like a press release for Evita Perón,
one of those tales that goes down
in countries where once a year
they haul the Virgin's statue
on a wagon and the hysterical poor
cover her with paper money the way
flies do sweet exudations.

Maybe you bargained with him:
The old Queen's on the way out.
Stick with me and you'll get
a stone cottage and be top hunter.
Just the truth, please,
the kind of information
that gives confidence
on the Subway: that we know
the right response to violence.
Was he, perhaps, unique;
and anyone else in the court
would, words or no, have had
your heart out, zip, and sizzling
on a stick, quick as a spark?
What's the Snow White approach
to paranoids, sociopaths
and sadists, the sure cure
for peer pressure? Or were you
just lucky?

Was there some threat:
The man I marry will be King
and if you lay a hand on me,
he'll have your skin? Or,
did your little hand whistle
through the air in a karate chop
that recalled to him
how tender is the groin?
Snow White, we don't want
to make the wrong move
when there's a sure-fire way
to handle the situation. What
do you say to keep the world
from having your heart out?

ANDREA HOLLANDER BUDY

Snow White

It was actually one of the dwarfs
who kissed her—Bashful,
who still won't admit it.
That is why she remained in the forest
with all of them and made up
the story of the prince. Otherwise,
wouldn't you be out there now
scavenging through wildflowers,
mistaking the footprints of your own
children for those little men?
And if you found some wild apples
growing in the thickest part, if no one
were looking, wouldn't you
take a bite? And pray
some kind of magic sleep
would snatch you
from the plainness
of your life?

KATHARYN HOWD MACHAN

Hazel Tells LaVerne

last night
im cleanin out my
howard johnsons ladies room
when all of a sudden
up pops this frog
musta come from the sewer
swimmin aroun an tryin ta
climb up the sida the bowl
so i goes ta flushm down
but sohelpmegod he starts talkin
bout a golden ball
an how i can be a princess
me a princess
well my mouth drops
all the way to the floor
an he says
kiss me just kiss me
once on the nose
well i screams
ya little green pervert
an i hitsm with my mop
an has ta flush
the toilet down three times
me
a princess

DONALD FINKEL

Sleeping Beauty

What is inescapable in this story   is the fact
that the thirteenth fairy   said what she said
'without greeting anyone   or even glancing
at the company'   the story goes further   it says
'she called out in a loud voice'   all that
about the twelfth fairy softening the curse
can be tossed aside   as a feeble attempt
to soothe the children   the twelve other fairies
for that matter   can be tossed aside   even the king
and the court   and the kingdom   can be tossed aside

What remains   is the old lady   no
even that can be tossed aside   what remains
is the woman   looking neither left nor right
what remains   is the loud voice saying
even if there is nobody to hear   'the Princess
shall prick herself with a distaff in her fifteenth year
and shall fall down dead'   there need in fact
not even be a princess

BARBARA HAMBY

Achtung, My Princess, Good Night

Arrivederci, Cinderella, your goose is cooked, grilled,
burned to be precise, blistered, while you, nestled in your

crumbling necropolis of love, think, who am I?
Delores del Rio? No, nothing so déclassé, yet

even your mice have deserted you, little pipsqueaks,
fled to serve your stepsisters, dedicated now to

good works, a soup kitchen, if you can imagine. What is this
heresy of ugliness that has overtaken the world?

I am Beauty, you scream. Wrong fairy tale, and
just so you don't forget, size sixes are not enough in this

karaoke culture, and even here you have to do more than
lip sync "Begin the Beguine," "My Funny Valentine,"

"Mona Lisa," "Satisfaction," because you can't get no,
no, no, no, consummation, so to speak. Sex is kaput,

over, married a decade, three litters of neurasthenic
princes, your figure shot, not to mention your vagina. Don't

quote me on that you cry, my public can't bear very much
reality. Who can? Yet there it is staring you in the face.

Scram, vamoose, la cucaracha, cha cha cha. Admit it, you're
tired of this creepy pedestal, the pressed pleats,

undercooked chicken, Prince Embonpoint and his cheesy
Virna Lisi look-alike mistress with her torpedo chest. Auf

Wiedersehen to this stinking fairy-tale life, this pack-rat
Xanadu built on the decomposing carcasses of girlish hope.

Yes, all your best friends, all your gorgeous diamonds are cubic
zirconias, but flashing like the real thing, as if you'd know.

9 ❦

EVER AFTER, OR A FEW YEARS LATER

what comes after happy?
WENDY TAYLOR CARLISLE

Forty years we've gone on dancing.
DOROTHY BARRESI

Nothing lasts.
LEE UPTON

DEBORA GREGER

Ever After

Youngest Brother, swan's wing
where one arm should be, yours the shirt
of nettles short a sleeve
and me with no time left to finish—
I didn't mend you all the way back into man
though I managed for your brothers;
they flit again from court to playing-courts
to courting while you station yourself,
wing folded from sight, avian eye
to the outside, no rebuke meant but love's.
Was it better then, the living on water,
the taking to air? I envied you.
When a king out hunting stumbled on me
in the nettle bed, I hid my blistered hands,
already promised to silence, to knitting us
back into family sting by sting.
Against his mime of marriage,
mine of no room for him was translated
as a tear-flooded dollhouse by our parents,
wept into his eddy of infatuation,
nothing left but for me to go to him,
bearing as trousseau the work cut out
into silence and your shirts.
I went gloved, and after dark, and lay by him,
still, hearing alongside his breath
something like wings far off.
So I told myself, and tried to recall my voice
as the nights shortened, warming to summer.
By day a pair of swans claimed the moat,
dipping and preening, the cob rolling
onto the pen's back, pinning her neck with his beak,
all too quickly over to drown her:
my fear the first time I saw it,
no martyr losing her footing down a bank,
just seamstress pricked by her own hand,
soothed by mud's dispassionate touch.
I suffered no unkindness—what then can I say to him

that I didn't more eloquently sign?
I envy you even the wing that maims you,
giving me, before you remember it,
a crippling half-hug. The swans' mute mating
until death, loss beaten to rage
strong enough to drag a sheep into water
and hold it under—how little
I've plumbed the nature of *happily.*

WENDY TAYLOR CARLISLE

Kissing the Frog

At the all-night pancake house,
the plastic seats cracked
and the water glasses etched
by 1000 washings, we connect
eagerly, hurried in from opposite directions,
pale and damp. At home,
we each have someone perfect
we can't trust—striped shirts, blond wrists.

Hunched over our cups, we remember
mouth-watering days at the river. Mayflies
hovered on slack eddies, the sun
leached all colors to olive drab.

Should I ask
if you still believe in wet kisses
rising to the surface like catfish?
Should I say I'm the same
hungry princess, prying at the menu
where I wish to find our story,
read it out loud and discover
what comes after happy?

Is it a picture of me lying on your chest,
that slithery touch?
Is it a kiss that changes your face?

Imagine us.
How it will be to open our ribs,
to gather in
the small, dark frogs.

RANDALL JARRELL

Cinderella

Her imaginary playmate was a grown-up
In sea-coal satin. The flame-blue glances,
The wings gauzy as the membrane that the ashes
Draw over an old ember—as the mother
In a jug of cider—were a comfort to her.
They sat by the fire and told each other stories.

"What men want. . . ." said the godmother softly—
How she went on it is hard for a man to say.
Their eyes, on their Father, were monumental marble.
Then they smiled like two old women, bussed each other,
Said, "Gossip, gossip"; and, lapped in each other's looks,
Mirror for mirror, drank a cup of tea.

Of cambric tea. But there is a reality
Under the good silk of the good sisters'
Good ball gowns. *She* knew. . . . Hard-breasted, naked-eyed,
She pushed her silk feet into glass, and rose within
A gown of imaginary gauze. The shy prince drank
A toast to her in champagne from her slipper

And breathed, "Bewitching!" Breathed, "I am bewitched!"
—She said to her godmother, "Men!"
And, later, looking down to see her flesh
Look back up from under lace, the ashy gauze
And pulsing marble of a bridal veil,
She wished it all a widow's coal-black weeds.

A sullen wife and a reluctant mother,
She sat all day in silence by the fire.
Better, later, to stare past her sons' sons,
Her daughters' daughters, and tell stories to the fire.
But best, dead, damned, to rock forever
Beside Hell's fireside—to see within the flames

The Heaven to whose gold-gauzed door there comes
A little dark old woman, the God's Mother,
And cries, "Come in, come in! My son's out now,
Out now, will be back soon, may be back never,
Who knows, eh? *We* know what they are—men, men!
But come, come in till then! Come in till then!"

DOROTHY BARRESI

Cinderella and Lazarus, Part II

> And all the question marks began singing of God's being.
> Tomas Tranströmer, "C Major"

"If the crown fits, wear it," the Prince always crowed.

Have a heart, the moon says now, the same one
the dish & the cow & the spoon
had dealings with.

One life's enough for anyone.

Did we mention that we began in ashes?
Bone-grave, small town,

our mourning mothers and sisters swatted back
the way a white horse
swats heat, sometimes hitting a fly;

later our gramophone, prized possession,
stiffened to a morning glory
with rigor mortis.
The wind roared like nothing in our ears, then nothing.
Kidney pills for kidney stones.

Forty years we've gone on dancing.
The shoe's on the other foot,
but we are always exactly the same couple

in original rags
older than God, than dirt,

doing the Lindy, the Bop, the oh
restless for consummation tango.
Not now death; but now, *now.*

Even his hands spoke in radical tongues.

MARLENE JOYCE PEARSON

Twenty Years After

for Ann Stanford

Twenty years after the ball
where she won the prince's heart,
her feet still small as a china doll's,
things were no longer a children's tale
with pumpkin coach and miraculous
mice transformed into white mares.
Twenty years after, she walked the shadowed halls
sipping white wine

while the prince—that eternal romantic, that spoiled son—
ran back to daddy's palace
carrying his catalogue, begging daddy
to order him another glass slipper.
Surely it would bring him a new lovely young lady,
one without saggy breasts, as Cindy had once been.

But Cinderella had grown up in ashes
and knew love's burn,
how dreams shatter like dropped crystal.
Even fairy godmother had died years ago.
And though she could sweep and clean
and sing like a swallow,
old prince charming would not
be wise as myth.

He was not content with her pure heart
and mortal love. He was no wizard.
He could not wipe the crow's feet from his own eyes
and his feet ached after a day at the courtyard.
Yet he clutched his dreams
like the drink she poured him when he came home,
gulping it down.

He would have three or four more before he could
face sleep. She knew he had no more power
than a mouse.
He was only a middle-aged man.

LOUISE GLÜCK

Gretel in Darkness

This is the world we wanted.
All who would have seen us dead
are dead. I hear the witch's cry
break in the moonlight through a sheet
of sugar: God rewards.
Her tongue shrivels into gas....

        Now, far from women's arms
and memory of women, in our father's hut
we sleep, are never hungry.
Why do I not forget?
My father bars the door, bars harm
from this house, and it is years.

No one remembers. Even you, my brother,
summer afternoons you look at me as though
you meant to leave,
as though it never happened.
But I killed for you. I see armed firs,
the spires of that gleaming kiln—

Nights I turn to you to hold me
but you are not there.
Am I alone? Spies
hiss in the stillness, Hansel,
we are there still and it is real, real,
that black forest and the fire in earnest.

AGHA SHAHID ALI

Hansel's Game

In those years I lived
happily ever after. And still do.
I played with every Gretel in town
including Gretel, my sister.

I walked into the forest,
trailing moon-sharpened pebbles
and traced back a route
from the grave to the womb.

Such stories end happily,
Mother said.

Darling, go out into the world,
the womb's no place for a big boy like you.

I wouldn't, I wouldn't.
She pushed
but I stuck on like gum.

So she baked garlic bread,
she knew I loved it.
And I dropped like a coin
once again into the world.

And again I walked into the forest,
lost in toadstools, thickets, ferns, and thorn,
and Gretel was hungry,

but I threw the bread,
crumb by crumb,
to light my route
from the womb to the grave.

When the moon rose,
the crumbs were gone.
A witch had to be somewhere near.

Well, I knew the ending,
I knew she would end badly,
a big boy now, I knew what witches do:
They drain big boys and ice them
with almonds and thick chocolate.

I didn't let her, I played innocent.

And Gretel and I lived
happily ever after. And still do:

We have a big ice-box
in our basement
where we keep the witch.

Now and then we take portions of her
to serve on special occasions.

And our old father washes
her blood from the dishes.

LEE UPTON

Snow White Over & Over

And her clavicle—
it is about a failure to kill.
A failure despite all methods.
It is like a guerrilla war
or a contest with insects.
The mirror violates everyone.
There is bacteria in the center
of the story of her throat—
a choking gasp—
something wanting triumph,
something to give itself over.
And still she won't die forever.
Nothing lasts.

ALICE FRIMAN

Snow White: The Prince

She was my perfection once—
An ivory heart
A white bud stopped in stone.
And because she'd never change
I could have filled cathedrals with my love.
My cold virgin. My wafer. My cup.

I did not count on the accident.
Or the children for that matter.
      Do you hear them?
    She'll play with them sometimes
    out in the fields. Her black hair
    streaked with gray, her waistline
    gone.
I cannot bear to look.

I like it better here.
This glass from Venice. It's very rare.
And this Egyptian ankh—symbol of life
Frozen in its own silence.
And this quaint piece:
The mirror from the old house. You must have
Heard of it. Go ahead. Study it if you wish.
I can't bear the way it makes me look—
  My eyes too close together
    dark blotches on my skin.
I'll say it needs to be re-silvered, but she won't have it.

She'll come at night sometimes
When she's alone.

I can't imagine what she sees.
Heaven only knows.

SUSAN MITCHELL

From the Journals of the Frog Prince

In March I dreamed of mud
sheets of mud over the ballroom chairs and table
rainbow slicks of mud under the throne.
In April I saw mud of clouds and mud of sun.
Now in May I find excuses to linger in the kitchen
for wafts of silt and ale
cinnamon and riverbottom
tender scallion and sour underlog.

At night I cannot sleep.
I am listening for the dribble of mud
climbing the stairs to our bedroom
as if a child in a wet bathing suit ran
up and down them in the dark.

Last night I said: Face it you're bored!
How many times can you live over with the same excitement
that moment when the princess leans
into the well her face a petal
falling to the surface of the water
as you rise like a bubble to her lips
the golden ball bursting from your mouth?
To test myself I said
remember how she hurled you against the wall
your body cracking open
skin shriveling to the bone
your small green heart splitting like a pod
and her face imprinted with every moment
of your transformation?

I no longer tremble.

Night after night I lie beside her.
"Why is your forehead so cool and damp?" she asks.
Her breasts are soft and dry as flour.
The hand that brushes my head is feverish.
At her touch I long for wet leaves
the slap of water against rocks.

"What are you thinking of?" she asks.
How can I tell her
I am thinking of the green skin
shoved like wet pants behind the Directoire desk?
Or tell her I am mortgaged to the hilt
of my sword, to the leek green tip of my soul?
Someday I will drag her by her hair
to the river—and what? Drown her?
Show her the green flame of my self rising at her feet?
But there's no more violence in her
than in a fence or a gate.

"What are you thinking of?" she whispers.
I am staring into the garden.
I am watching the moon
wind its trail of golden slime around the oak,
over the stone basin of the fountain.
How can I tell her
I am thinking that transformations are not forever?

ANNE SHELDON

The Prince Who Woke Briar Rose

He talks too much, according to her brother.
She, however, knows the Prince's blather
for the outward audible sign of waking life.
And she's no angel, either, with a cold
unpleasant knot left from too much sleep.
But somehow she grew up, asleep, and knew
the nervous Prince for what he was, although
she didn't see the crimson brambles shrinking
from his boots. Or all those other princes
moldering inside the house-high thicket—
athletes, poets, scholars, warriors—how
he wondered, could he be the chosen man?
Smart enough to keep on walking, he was
strong enough to force the attic door.

For his unspeaking mouth, her eyes broke open.
Or was it more than just a kiss? the shaking
of the bed? the Prince for once voracious,
pushing, missing, finally coming home?
Whatever. They were married after breakfast.

Married now twelve years and King for three,
he still can't take it in. At banquets, fairs,
he talks of how it feels to be the One,
describes the varied sleepers in the Hall:
the cook with greasy spoon upraised to strike
the scullion, the spaniel poised to scratch,
the manicurist and the Queen. Cobwebs?
Interesting. No worse than you'd expect—
the spiders slept as well.

She studies, while he speaks, the borderland
beneath his chin where beard begins and where
it deepens. He is her unenchanted landscape,
the woods and hills and gullies of the world
she missed those hundred dateless winters.
She sleeps a different sleep beside her Prince,

from which, for certain years and days, she'll wake
each ordinary morning to a whiff
of coffee, briefly fresh, the ticking clock,
a splash of moving sun across the panes.

PAMELA WHITE HADAS

Queen Charming Writes Again

for Alice, yet another revision

A woman writing thinks back through her mothers.
Virginia Woolf

Dear Godmother,
                              Another year, and today
Charmingshire's Serendipity Rendezvous
Ball rolls round again, with all my festive duties
of gratitude; thus, my annual letter to you.
I wish you could see the gorgeous pumpkin taxi

I've ordered for my Good Will Progress (dim
patch, though stable, on your conjured coupe). I'll visit
the village, street hovel I once called home.
The house has its blue plaque now. I remember it
as "modest," but now it's disgraceful—a slum!

I guess the present tenants dress in rags and smear
their faces with soot just to try to catch *my* eye,
as if a mere grubby urchin caught yours! I'm sure
all year they're clean, neat, and happy as everybody
back then but me. I was more than your lazy beggar,

I'd like to shout. I was a *real* princess at heart.
Can I tell them they have to do more than mope
for *my* money? Can't the luckless do more than look hurt?
How vile, this charity business! There's no glib escape,
I'd like to tell them: learn to pander, stoop to flirt.

And yet, as I muse on going back, the twitchy
footmice and Pega-soused rats you reorganized
for my swell-cum-clodpate courtship pageantry
debut still run loose and wild in my galvanized
pasture of nightmares. I wonder: Why do they

have more reality than the King? Don't tell
me you're just reminding me how much I owe
to your clout behind the scenes. Your pure goodwill

I can't quite believe in anymore. So what if now
I just said: "no": A rotten job, being royal.

Would I get my own back? Would I look like *them?*
Or would I indulge in the same old song and dance,
only, this time around, to lose? The snickers come
like flocks of moths at night. No daily circumstance
compares, bears thinking of…Yet, I grow numb

with satisfactions. Do many of your pets
come back asking for trouble like this, or am I
doomed to the unforgivable peeves and snits
of my not-I underclass? Where is the charity
of your original senses, of humor and limit?

Have I mislaid so much? My maiden nickname
still flutters in the dark, scantling, recherché,
whisking and shushing—its tatty, ashen rhythm
around my heart, still driven to the tune of seedy
axles, fare-meter's click-cluck time; about time…

But come morning, my royal pseudo- (or is it alter-?)
nym comes back to me, to stir me from my tangled bed.
I wake, and see reverted Pumpkin take to the air
in streaks of distant reflection, distant cloud.
I hear the King's footsteps, and then his tap at my door.

He brings a breakfast tray—such a sweetie, really.
I have nothing to complain of there, unless
of his unremitting kindness, an idiotic, saintly
charm binding me to our secret undeservingness.
I wiggle my toes, still almost numb from my crazy

nightlong jigging in your hallucinatorium.
They feel half-slippered still, one see-through strap
of solid tears wearing thin. I kick to free them
for the daily round, prosaic as my shining cup
of tea. I pour a steady, miraculous stream

of glitters, strained to absolute clarity,
golden as silence, hospitable to cloud. Lemon
or milk? I stare into the cup, past the glimmery

ghost's breath on the surface…Mother?…Gone.
The King bends to kiss me good-morning. "Silly,"

he whispers, "time to rise and shine, drink up before
it's cold. We've got a big day ahead of us."
Oh, yes, the flowers, the pastries, last-minute palaver
and fidgets over the guest list…And so I dress,
put on my manners, my face, my workaday collar

and coronet. I check my regalia, pressed and hung straight
for the evening's do. All day I'm Queen, charming to boot,
but even on such a royal day, as you know…midnight
strikes me hard, dumps my brain right back in the ashbucket,
glad rags and all. But of course you know. You wait

at the garden hedge, call softly…We happen all over
again. I swallow my doubts and fetch an unlikely
squash. I watch my sooty creep-mouse pinafore
dissolve, revise, riddle over with a finery
to equal my envy. I see mice evolve to power,

each tiny hack capacity harnessed somehow
under your wand. Everything you do to disguise
me, right down to the oddity of the transparent shoe,
is supposed to make me more or less myself, I guess.
But which? Without the punctual nightmare, could the show

go on? Could you take it from me? Could you let me stop
the rehearsals—sorting the lentils from ashes, my guilty
visits to the hazelnut tree, to keep
the crooked breeze green by Mother's grave? Will I
forever fall for Narcissus' echo, clap-

trappedly snapping up rejection to re-cinder
my nest? Do you keep me at this to improve
my character, or intend to turn your back-burner
simmer down to silence soon? Please forgive
my confusion—bad enough to need another

spectacular rescue, but not deserve the same.
My wonder ripens, despite the years of cool satin.
The windfall, the sunrise reprieve does come

to some felons convicted, even she who's done in
the child she was expecting...to be...This is as

(unclear—I'm sorry—*but you know what I mean*—

if anyone could.) Do our humiliating pangs
of separation ever soften? Today, We hold an audience,
the King and I, for all our subjects—their hopes, harangues,
tragic or funny stories—noblesse oblige!—each grievance
attended, assuaged. And *then,* of course, the flings

and curtsies of the dance. Have you scoured the countryside
for someone my grown son might see fit to marry?
He's ready, and if she works out, I shall take her aside
and promise her no change but constancy's.
She'll know I'm a witch, your opposite, and need

to regard me, if at all, as I did my own stepmother,
bless her hearth. Let's hope for one who wants not
to change the world too loudly. Someday let her
enjoy her babies and fetes, write you a thank-you note
as pleasing as should be, more than I can muster.

All who chance to enter into the state of Charming,
I'd tell her, are charged with a possible grace,
a tentative keeping—of promise, houses, time
and with luck, a sense of humor, figure, face
that can fall and lift again, to pray or scream...

As never, ever,

Your "Cinderella"

RONALD KOERTGE

Gretel

said she didn't know anything about ovens
so the witch crawled in to show her
and Bam! went the big door.

Then she strolled out to the shed where
her brother was fattening, knocked down
a wall and lifted him high in the air.

Not long after the adventure in the forest
Gretel married so she could live happily.
Her husband was soft as Hansel. Her
husband liked to eat. He liked to see
her in the oven with the pies and cakes.

Ever after was the size of a kitchen.
Gretel remembered when times were better.
She laughed out loud when the witch
popped like a weenie.

"Gretel! Stop fooling around and fix
my dinner."

"There's something wrong with this oven,"
she says, her eyes bright as treasure.
"Can you come here a minute?"

AGHA SHAHID ALI

An Interview with Red Riding Hood,
Now No Longer Little

How dark it was inside the wolf!
Red Riding Hood in Grimm

Q. Whatever happened after
   the wolf died?

A. My father, a self-made man,
   he made good.
   Mind you, no ordinary woodsman,
   he slowly bought the whole forest,
   had it combed for wolves.
   Had it cut down.
   But the wolves escaped,
   like guerillas, into
   the mountains.
   He owns a timber industry.
   I, of course, am an heiress.

Q. And your grandma?

A. She had nightmares.
   She'd wake up crying, "Wolf! Wolf!"
   We had to put her in a home.
   I took her baskets of fruit,
   flowers, cakes, wines.
   Always in the red velvet cap.
   I got sick of lisping for her,
   "Grandma, what big eyes you have!"
   That always made her laugh.
   The last time I saw her, she cried,
   "Save me, he's coming to eat me up!"
   We gave her a quiet burial.

Q. Do you have any regrets?

A. Yes.
   I lied when I said it was dark.
   Now I drive through the city,
   hearing wolves at every turn.
   How warm it was inside the wolf!

MAXINE KUMIN

The Archaeology of a Marriage

When Sleeping Beauty wakes up
she is almost fifty years old.
Time to start planning her retirement cottage.
The Prince in sneakers stands thwacking
his squash racquet. He plays
three nights a week at his club,
it gets the heart action up.
What *he* wants in the cottage
is a sauna and an extra-firm Beauty-
rest mattress, which *she* sees as an exquisite
sarcasm directed against her long slumber.
Was it *her* fault he took so long
to hack his way through the brambles?
Why didn't he carry a chainsaw
like any sensible woodsman?
Why, for that matter, should any
twentieth-century woman
have to lie down at the prick of
a spindle etcetera etcetera
and he is stung to reply
in kind and soon they are at it.

If only they could go back to
the simplest beginnings. She
remembers especially a snapshot
of herself in a checked gingham outfit.
He is wearing his Navy dress whites.
She remembers the illicit weekend
in El Paso, twenty years before
illicit weekends came out of the closet.
Just before Hiroshima
just before Nagasaki
they nervously straddled the border
he an ensign on a forged three-day pass
she a technical virgin from Boston.
What he remembers is vaster:
something about his whole future

compressed to a stolen weekend.
He was to be shipped out tomorrow
for the massive land intervention.
He was to have stormed Japan.
Then, merely thinking of dying
gave him a noble erection.

Now, thanatopsis is calmer,
the first ripe berry on the stem,
a loss leader luring his greedy
hands deeper into the thicket
than he has ever been.
Deeper than he cares to be.
At the sight of the castle, however,
he recovers his wits and backtracks
meanwhile picking. Soon his bucket
is heavier etcetera than ever
and he is older etcetera
and still no spell has been recast
back at Planned Acres Cottage.
Each day he goes forth to gather
small fruits. Each evening she stands
over the stewpot skimming
the acid foam from the jam
expecting to work things out
awaiting, you might say, a unicorn
her head stuffed full of old notions
and the slotted spoon in her hand.

10

LIVING THE TALES

what I see
Is not a fairy tale, but life
AMY LOWELL

like Gretel looking back
JEFF WALT

We live today those stories we were told.
DIANE THIEL

GREGORY ORR

Two Lines from the Brothers Grimm

Now we must get up quickly,
dress ourselves, and run away.
Because it surrounds us, because
they are coming with wolves on leashes,
because I stood just now at the window
and saw the wall of hills on fire.

They have taken our parents away.
Downstairs in the half dark, two strangers
move about, lighting the stove.

EMILY HIESTAND

The Old Story

The wish that every touched thing turn gold
is chaos in morning light; logic hunkers
and plain words mean nothing over toast.
What can be recalled . . . straw to silk,
gilded birds, a forest with snow
and more snow falling. And morning is gone.

The youngest prince, lacking title,
forsakes the palace and soon is lost in a wood.
And the princess, who speaks to frogs,
strays from insufferable suitors, the embroidery.
Their minds are a thicketwood,
patches of light in gorgeous fretwork, given

to pity for the siblings who jostle
in coaches to their coronations, who wander
swell in lugubrious forests.
Everyone can be in the story—the elected,
the popular and well-to-do.
And it may happen in a grocery store—

every shopper with Bird's Eye peas
a princess with a pocketful of magic,
loose in a world that quavers with ash
and a grace not much involved with merit.
Soon comes an encounter with something
like death, and the character changes to stone.

But at last we hear no more of unearthly beauty;
the acrid stone assumes a mortal shape
and laundry whirls like seasons as now,
everyday, grey as bankers or blue as jazz,
we kiss our collection of toads.

MARK DeFOE

Daughters with Toad

Unblinking thing, as absolute as clay.
Fumed from the dank by my mower's snarl, he muses.
My daughters find him, and their squeals propel,
bounce him from his mope, ringing him with glee.

With sly, leery touch they probe his apathy
unearthed—half-thrown, with lurching, bloated thump
he falls. They toy and stroke, forgive his piss,
his pebbled hide, coo to his bulbous stare.

Squat in their palms, he thrills them with his pulse.
They lean near, enraptured by his ugliness,
wild hair burnished down round him in bright waves.
And they whisper, foreheads almost touching.

Then each brings her lips to meet that grim crack
of torpid mouth. They return him to grass
to await the kisses' transformation.
Nothing. The pale throat only swells the air

and flutters, emits one pathetic croak.
They laugh, and to the toad their teeth so fine
must gleam like the teeth of little foxes.
Uneaten, he ponders on, abandoned.

My daughters are not sad. The day will be
husband enough, obedient to whim—
a royal ball. They waltz toward lunchtime,
assuring me he spoke to them in Prince.

MARTHA RONK

Dock

for my nephew, Jonathan

Dock he tells me isn't what we're walking on
but in *Snow White* he remembers the eyeglasses
and how can we fish from it, myopic, unsteady
as I remember the roses on the wallpaper at night
hatching birds with open eye. Sing is what
the water does and mosquitoes on the backs of knees
he peels a bandage from covered in Disney bits
which wheel his mind like trucks he takes to bed
imprinted on cheeks and hands as he grabs mine
to steady his step into the rowboat from which
he sees a forest he wants to row into the darkest part of.

AMY LOWELL

A Fairy Tale

On winter nights beside the nursery fire
We read the fairy tale, while glowing coals
Builded its pictures. There before our eyes
We saw the vaulted hall of traceried stone
Uprear itself, the distant ceiling hung
With pendent stalactites like frozen vines;
And all along the walls at intervals,
Curled upwards into pillars, roses climbed,
And ramped and were confined, and clustered leaves
Divided where there peered a laughing face.
The foliage seemed to rustle in the wind,
A silent murmur, carved in still, gray stone.
High pointed windows pierced the southern wall
Whence proud escutcheons flung prismatic fires
To stain the tessellated marble floor
With pools of red, and quivering green, and blue;
And in the shade beyond the further door,
Its sober squares of black and white were hid
Beneath a restless, shuffling, wide-eyed mob
Of lackeys and retainers come to view
The Christening.
A sudden blare of trumpets, and the throng
About the entrance parted as the guests
Filed singly in with rare and precious gifts.
Our eager fancies noted all they brought,
The glorious unattainable delights!
But always there was one unbidden guest
Who cursed the child and left it bitterness.

The fire falls asunder, all is changed,
I am no more a child, and what I see
Is not a fairy tale, but life, my life.
The gifts are there, the many pleasant things:
Health, wealth, long-settled friendships, with a name
Which honors all who bear it, and the power
Of making words obedient. This is much;
But overshadowing all is still the curse,
That never shall I be fulfilled by love!

Along the parching highroad of the world
No other soul shall bear mine company.
Always shall I be teased with semblances,
With cruel impostures, which I trust awhile
Then dash to pieces, as a careless boy
Flings a kaleidoscope, which shattering
Strews all the ground about with coloured shards.
So I behold my visions on the ground
No longer radiant, an ignoble heap
Of broken, dusty glass. And so, unlit,
Even by hope or faith, my dragging steps
Force me forever through the passing days.

MEG KEARNEY

Fundevogel

> *Fundevogel, do not forsake me, and*
> *I will never forsake you.*
> The Brothers Grimm

Perhaps father is another word
for sleep. My dead father sleeps
without rest, crossing between

this life and the last. My blood
father sleeps in Florida, or
Budapest, or anywhere I am not.

In his sleep my dead father glides
through my window. He is young
again; I sit on his lap while he reads

The Frog Prince and *Fundevogel*,
the foundling baby carried away
by a bird. In his world, my dead

father reads the Brothers Grimm.
We dream up a happy ending.
In Boca Raton, my blood father

dreams, feverish, grinding his teeth,
murmuring a story that his wife,
propped on her elbow in bed,

has been straining for years to
catch. By watching him she knows
when the dream is about to end:

he twitches, swallows, says, Come
back. But always the woman
and the little girl are walking hand-

in-hand into the forest. He opens
his mouth, closes it. He does not
know their names. This is where

the story ends. He wakes up. My
dead father goes grey in my room,
closes his book, kisses my forehead.

Margaret, he says, it's time to sleep.
I will be his good girl after the meddle-
some hawk follows him out the window.

CHARLES MARTIN

A Happy Ending for the Lost Children

One of their picture books would no doubt show
The two lost children wandering in a maze
Of anthropomorphic tree limbs: the familiar crow

Swoops down upon the trail they leave of corn,
Tolerant of the error of their ways.
Hand in hand they stumble onto the story,

Brighteyed with beginnings of fever, scared
Half to death, yet never for a moment
Doubting the outcome that had been prepared

Long in advance: Girl saves brother from oven,
Appalling witch dies in appropriate torment;
Her hoarded treasure buys them their parents' love.

＊　＊　＊

"As happy an ending as any fable
Can provide," squawks the crow, who had expected more:
Delicate morsels from the witch's table.

It's an old story—in the modern version
The random children fall to random terror.
You see it nightly on the television:

The yellow tape that winds its way around
The lop-eared bear, the plastic ukulele, shattered
In a fit of rage—lost children now are found

In the first place where we would think to look:
Under the fallen leaves, under the scattered
Pages of a lost children's picture book.

＊　＊　＊

But if we leave terror waiting in the rain
For the wrong bus, or if we have terror find,
At the very last moment the right train,

Only to get off at the wrong station—
If we for once imagine a happy ending,
Which is, as always, a continuation,

It's because the happy ending's a necessity,
It isn't just a sentimental ploy—
Without the happy ending there would be

No one to tell the story to but the witch,
And the story is clearly meant for the girl and boy
Just now about to step into her kitchen.

PETER COOLEY

Nocturne with Witch, Oven and Two Little Figures

Haphazardly a blizzard collects over our window
as if the moon, weaving between clouds, were breathing it.

In the same window seat, stitched with lilies, each minute prickly,
in which she read me fifty-five years back

her favorite, "Hansel and Gretel,"
I am reading to my sister the same tale tonight.

She is sixty-eight, I am fifty-eight.
Now when she fidgets, as if from inattention,

I slam *The Brothers Grimm* down on her head
just as she slammed me at three, spitting a word

like a black worm I spit back at her. I shake her, screaming
if she dares to cry or tell our mother or father

I will come into her room at midnight
as I did last night dressed as The Boogie Man,

a pair of scissors in my hand to cut her weenie off.
But I don't have one, stupid, she laughs, shrilly

and it is her voice from age thirteen, a voice-over
of her voice now, post-menopausal, grating over it.

Here the book cracks open, we step into it,
the wood stretches before us, gnarled, primeval

and we are hand in hand as our real parents planned
we should be in their version of the tale

where brother and sister adventure with a good witch,
something like the old maid fifth grade teacher

my sister and I shared, dwarfed, hunchbacked,
always in black and chalk-enshrouded

because she crashed erasers together like cymbals, grinning
while she crashed unceasingly, beaming, scolding a class,

or if there were a bad witch for them she was a teacher
of moral precept stiff and upright as the paddling sticks

I suffered, just like my sister, a stiff dose of weekly
at Bushnell Congregational Sunday School.

Now as the dream continues, I shrink, sprout wings
until I am a tiny raven, I fly atop a tree.

My sister trundles on, happy without me, toward the witch's house,
little aware that what awaits her, ravenous, magical

is a shadow of herself, spectral in the doorway
and after she sates herself with delicious architecture

she will enter in to be devoured by herself,
witch and sister one in the pot brought to a boil

in this, the other life, where I am author.

NICOLE COOLEY

Snow White

The casket lengthens with her body
in the story told by the two sisters,
storytellers of the unnamed village
where the Brothers Grimm stop for the night.

Listen, the first says, she was warned
not to open the door to anyone and three times
she invited the mad woman in, let

The Queen lace the corset to crush the breath
from her body, placed the poison comb
in her own black hair, swallowed
a piece from the magic side of the apple.

At the table in the sisters' house the men
translate each word into their own language.
The sisters' story fills page after page.

In this story, the women are condemned
to daylight, the Queen dancing the fire
dance in iron shoes, the Queen burning.
The girl's body is locked in the Prince's embrace.

Years later, in another country, my mother's sisters
accept the apple like a communion wafer:
the Body of Christ, the Bread of Heaven.

At the altar they wait, hands open, hoping
to sleep for the rest of the century while they grow
old in their deaths, apart from everyone,
and beg the Queen to return with the other

punishments, greater terrors, a promise—
this time, nothing will save you.
If they drink from the Cup of Salvation,

they can refuse the Prince and his offer
of refuge, his kingdom. In the forest
I wash my aunts' faces with wine and water.
I lay their bodies on the crystal slab.

Their eyes stay open. Nothing can carry them
into the sleep they want. Over and over I prepare
the potion to take the sisters into the other world.

They can't get enough of oblivion.

ELLINE LIPKIN

Conversation with My Father

after Grimm's "The Maiden Without Hands"

After we speak, I go to the hardware store
to decide on a drill, feel each black-packaged tool
bristle with its will to do harm. I interlope
among bit sets, arrays of blade and shaft,
gun-like metal shapes that brag of power.
The word-whir of our talk still buzzes like
a saw always left in a corner, ready to hack.
Important—safety instructions flutter then drop.
I follow your advice on what's needed to needle
a skin of paint, the force it takes to punch the wall.

How much better if I could have been like Athena,
springing clear as a doe, neat as a sum,
blasted out of your head like a sweep of clean logic.
If only I could have been pure as a product
of the mind's mitosis, justified as when
'if' begets 'then,' and 'a' equals 'c,'
each chamber of reason I passed
smelting an iron-ore layer over my breast.
How alike we could be when I emerged,
balanced as an axiom, threaded straight as a theory,
and born armed, with bow and arrow in hand.

Instead, in your grip, Thumbelina, a glass angel,
a set of porcelain arms crossed behind a back.
My hand was to stay undissolved as a spun-sugar lump
until asked for, approved of, then towed down an aisle.
We come again to the oldest version of this story,
but I've told you I can't be good as Grimm's girl,
when we stand near the ax I draw my wrists back,
I won't let you bronze the cut cups of my palms.

ESTHA WEINER

Transfiguration Begins at Home

The "Cinderella Staircase" divided upstairs
from downstairs   its curves of elegance
branded early on the child   who turned it
into a story   over   and over again
The person who started at the top   was
never the person   who reached the bottom
The one who climbed it   from the bottom was
always different at the top   Cinderella
could turn into a princess   A prince could
turn into a frog   Before a father could
descend it with a daughter on his arm
to give her away   in marriage   a daughter
would ascend it   with a father on her arm
to give him away   to silence   Anything
is possible

YUSEF KOMUNYAKAA

Castrato

You've made me Little Red
Riding Hood. Mister Wolf
Has my scent on his breath,
& I've forgotten how to bluff

Shadows back into the hedgerow.
The same contralto is in my throat
Year after year. But the scalpel
Is what I remember most. Please note

This: hymns die on my tongue
Before they can heal.
Smooth as my sister's doll baby
Down there, I don't know how I feel

Or need. Entangled in so many
What-ifs. Neither north nor south.
I wish I knew how to stop women
From crying when I open my mouth.

JAMES NOLAN

Poem About Straw

for Ginny

I shut you in my bed that night
like the princess in the castle
to spin my room of straw to gold
with your wide hips   love's handles.
Spinning-jenny   cotton ginny
we spun all night to turn
the straw to bolts of gold
that streamed in through the window

at dawn when the princess changed
her last straw to coin for the king
and the Jews rose to mix the batch
of straw to brick for Pharaoh's tomb
in the desert where the camel's back
was broken by that last straw and he
leapt through the eye of a needle
moving mustard seeds and mountains
of straw
hats and alligator shoes
the princess wore

on the beach   after breakfast
when we walked hand to handle
straw wound with gold in our hair.

RACHEL HADAS

The Wolf in the Bed

From when you still could see,
do you remember the print beside your bed?
Doré's "Red Riding Hood":
the wide-eyed little girl
shares a pillow with the bonneted
beast. Recall the sidelong
look that links the child
and the shaggy monster
snuggling beside her.
Blankets pulled to their chins
conceal the tangled matters underneath:
a secret region, shadowy deep forest
through which a covered basket
is being carried, bread and wine
and books to the sick one's bedside.
You are the girl in bed beside the beast
or you're the grandmother, I visit you—
but no, since it's my mother, too, who's dying.
Is she in bed with you, since both are breathed on,
crowded, jostled by the restless wolf?
Now I arrive and climb in with you both
(the wolf makes room for me a little while)
and gingerly, so as not
to jar your various lifelines,
cradle you in my arms, my friend, my mother,
and read you stories of children
walking unattended through dark woods.

RACHEL HADAS

The Sleeping Beauty

Husk of a person beyond summer's pale,
the sleeping beauty dreaded to be woken
even by affection. The moon's veil
shrouded what little sky high monuments
(overgrown themselves by brambles) let
filter through. The spells had all been spoken.
Was it cruel or merciful to move
even a finger closer to the still
deeply breathing figure on the dais,
his slumber royal and illegible?

> Under layers of dust I glimpsed your face.
> As if our year of stories had alighted
> on those shut lips and would at the right word
> emerge and fly into the common air,
> I bent: to catch a signal? Steal a kiss
> never in the first place mine to take?
> Was I there to give or to receive?
> As soon as I approached, you seemed to stir,
> as who should ward off a too early waking.
> A pulse like hope beat blood into your cheeks.

The cornered moon sent grayish gleams of dim
illumination down—or transformation?
What would he do or say if he awoke?
Given new life, what would he become?
As I watched, the momentary motion
subsided, and the dream began again,
blanketing him for another year,
another hundred years, when he might wake
(sunlight and breakfast and the table set)
tuned to a kiss still drying on his lips—

a kiss of friendship and the key to freedom,
expanse of future, time's apportionment
to ordinary mornings, noons, and nights.
All this lay in the world of slender chances
suspended from a filament of breath
severed each second by the blade of danger.
Say you slept a hundred years, then woke
cured but bewildered to an empty world
to take your chances in, with years to spare.
I kiss you. Cured: the word hangs there like smoke.

MARLENE JOYCE PEARSON

This Is a Convalescent Home, Not the Fairy Tale Cottage and Always the Good Father

for Aunt Stella, January 26, 1913–March 2, 1989

Lunch cart squeaks to my old aunt's room,
stops by the side of her bed. A green tray
chipped on the edge

like the nurse's front tooth, the white-haired
nurse who lifts bent metal cover. Smell
of cheese slithers out stringy like rope
and knots in the air. My aunt cannot eat.
Fingers the corn instead. Kernels drop
to the floor. She says she is losing

a pound a day, pokes a grayish-blue finger
through metal bars on the bed, lets me feel
her knuckle as if I am the witch and she Hansel
in this oven they call a convalescent home.

I am not the reason she is dying. I hold her
hand like Gretel, lost too in this forest.
Her fingers cling to mine like passion
vine to tree. She hears her father
though he's been dead thirty years, smells
hot chocolate in his kitchen. When she yells,
"I want two marshmallows dad," the nurse walks
in, arms scissoring like garden shears. I am afraid

she will cut us apart. Instead, large hands
fluff my aunt's pillow against bosom
like any good mother while I count corn kernels
on the tray, the ones my aunt has dropped
to the floor. The nurse picks up a few

before she leaves, kicks two out into the hall.
My aunt is dropping more. Pale yellow
kernels lie on the floor like a code—
secret seeds to lead the children home.

JEFF WALT

Like Gretel

I wanted to be the first
to go. Not the strong one
left behind squinting
away winter light,
scattering ashes blessed
with prayers I do not understand—
handfuls of you
on the wet snow. And me,
like Gretel looking back
at the trail of ash, my tracks
following me deeper
into the dark wood.

LISEL MUELLER

Reading the Brothers Grimm to Jenny

Dead means somebody has to kiss you.

Jenny, your mind commands
kingdoms of black and white:
you shoulder the crow on your left
the snowbird on your right;
for you the cinders part
and let the lentils through,
and noise falls into place
as screech or sweet roo-coo,
while in my own, real world
gray foxes and gray wolves
bargain eye to eye,
and the amazing dove
takes shelter under the wing
of the raven to keep dry.

Knowing that you must climb,
one day, the ancient tower
where disenchantment binds
the curls of innocence,
that you must live with power
and honor circumstance,
that choice is what comes true—
O, Jenny, pure in heart,
why do I lie to you?

Why do I read you tales
in which birds speak the truth
and pity cures the blind,
and beauty reaches deep
to prove a royal mind?
Death is a small mistake
there, where the kiss revives;
Jenny, we make just dreams
out of our unjust lives.

Still, when your truthful eyes,
your keen, attentive stare,
endow the vacuous slut
with royalty, when you match
her soul to her shimmering hair,
what can she do but rise
to your imagined throne?
And what can I, but see
beyond the world that is
when, faithful, you insist
I have the golden key—
and learn from you once more
the terror and the bliss,
the world as it might be?

DIANE THIEL

Kinder- und Hausmärchen

tiefere Bedeutung
Liegt in dem Märchen meiner Kinderjahre
Als in der Wahrheit, die das Leben lehrt.
Friedrich Schiller

deeper meaning
lies in the fairy tales of my childhood
than in the truth that life teaches.

Saint Nikolaus had a giant gunny sack
to put the children in if they were bad.
It was a hole so deep you'd never come back.
A porch swing full of stories, where the smoke
went up in hot, concentric, perfect rings
and filled our heads with unbelievable things.

A nursery heavy with history
where nothing was whatever it had seemed,
where Aschenputtel's sisters cut their feet
half off—so desperate they were to fit.
And in the end, they also lost their eyes
when steel-grey birds descended from the skies.

Rotkäppchen's wolf was someone that she knew,
who wooed her with a man's words in the woods.
But she escaped. It always struck me most
how Grandmother, whose world was swallowed whole,
leapt fully formed out of the wolf alive.
Her will came down the decades to survive

in mine—my heart still desperately believes
the stories where somebody re-conceives
herself, emerges from the hidden belly,
the warring home dug deep inside the city.
We live today those stories we were told.
*Es war einmal im tiefen tiefen Wald.**

*Once upon a time in the deep deep wood.

ABOUT THE AUTHORS

AGHA SHAHID ALI (1949–2001), a noted translator as well as poet, was born in New Delhi, India, grew up in Kashmir, and emigrated to the US in his early twenties. His books include *Rooms Are Never Finished* (Norton, 2001), *The Country Without a Post Office* (Norton, 1997), *A Nostalgist's Map of America* (Norton, 1991), and *The Half-Inch Himalayas* (Wesleyan, 1987).

JULIA ALVAREZ was born in the Dominican Republic and emigrated to the US in 1960. Her books of poetry include *The Other Side/El Otro Lado* (Dutton, 1995) and *Homecoming* (Grove, 1984; Plume, 1996, rev. ed). She has also published several novels including *How the Garcia Girls Lost Their Accents, In the Time of Butterflies,* and *In the Name of Salomé.*

MARGARET ATWOOD was born in Ottawa, Canada. She is the author of numerous books of poetry and prose. Her most recent collections of poetry are *Morning in the Burned House* (Houghton Mifflin, 1995), *Selected Poems II 1976–1986,* and *Selected Poems 1965–1975.* Her novels include *Surfacing, The Handmaid's Tale,* and *The Blind Assassin.*

MARY JO BANG is the author of three books of poems: *Apology for Want* (Univ. Press New England, 1997), *Louise in Love* (Grove, 2001), and *The Downstream Extremity of the Isle of Swans* (Georgia, 2001). She has been poetry editor of *Boston Review* since 1995 and currently teaches at Washington University, St. Louis, MO.

CAROL JANE BANGS, a fourth-generation Oregonian, is author of *The Bones of the Earth* (New Directions, 1982) and *Irreconcilable Differences* (Confluence Press, 1978). Her poems are included in *The Norton Introduction to Poetry, Ravishing DisUnities: Real Ghazals in English,* and other anthologies and textbooks. She lives on Marrowstone Island, Washington.

ALIKI BARNSTONE was born in New Haven and grew up in Bloomington, Indiana. Her most recent books are *Madly in Love* (Carnegie Mellon, 1997) and *Wild With It* (Sheep Meadow, 2002). She edited *Voices of Light: Spiritual Poems by Women from Around the World from Ancient Sumeria to Now* (Shambhala, 1999), and is a professor at the University of Nevada, Las Vegas.

DOROTHY BARRESI is the author of *All of the Above* (Beacon, 1991), *The Post-Rapture Diner* (Pittsburgh, 1995), winner of an American Book Award, and *Rouge Pulp* (Pittsburgh, 2002). She is professor of English at California State University, Northridge, and lives in Los Angeles.

ERIN BELIEU has two books of poetry from Copper Canyon Press: *One Above & One Below* (2000) and *Infanta* (1995). She is coeditor, with Susan Aizenberg, of the anthology *The Extraordinary Tide: New Poetry by American Women* (Columbia, 2001), and she teaches in the creative writing program of Ohio University.

BRUCE BENNETT was born in Philadelphia. He is the author of *Straw Into Gold* (Cleveland State, 1984), *I Never Danced with Mary Beth* (Foothills, 1991), *Taking Off* (Orchises, 1992), and *Navigating the Distances: Poems New and Selected* (Orchises, 1999). He is Director of Creative Writing and of the Wells College Book Arts Center at Wells College, Aurora, NY, where he has taught since 1973.

OLGA BROUMAS is the author of several books of poetry including *Beginning with O*, which won the Yale Younger Poets Prize (Yale, 1977), *Perpetua* (Copper Canyon, 1990), and most recently *Rave: Poems 1975–1999* (Copper Canyon, 1999). She is also a noted translator of Greek poet Odysseas Elytis.

ANDREA HOLLANDER BUDY is the author of *House Without a Dreamer* (Story Line, 1993) and *The Other Life* (Story Line, 2001). She has also written for the theater and is a frequent book reviewer. Since 1991 she has been the Writer-in-Residence at Lyon College, Batesville, AR, where she was awarded the Lamar Williamson Prize for Excellence in Teaching.

EMMA BULL is the author of *War for the Oaks, Bone Dance,* and other fantasy novels. She has also collaborated with her husband, Will Shetterly, on screenplays. Her current band, the Flash Girls, released their third album, *Play Each Morning, Wild Queen,* in 2001. She lives in N. Hollywood, California.

REGIE CABICO was born in Baltimore, Maryland. His work appears in several anthologies including *Bum Rush the Page: Def Poetry Jam, The Outlaw Bible of American Poetry,* and *The World in Us: Gay & Lesbian Poets of the Next Wave.* A poetry slam champion, he appeared on HBO's *Def Poetry Jam 2* and *In the Life* on PBS.

MIKE CARLIN teaches creative writing and satire at Bucknell University, where he is an interim editor of *West Branch* magazine. His poems have appeared in *Bakunin, Onthebus, Evansville Review, Sheila-na-Gig,* and elsewhere. He has been a California poet-in-the-schools and poet-in-residence at the Pasadena Public Library.

PATRICIA CARLIN was born and lives in New York City. She is the author of *Original Green* (Marsh Hawk Press, 2003). Her work has appeared in *Verse, Boulevard, American Letters & Commentary,* and other journals. She is an editor of *Barrow Street* and cofounder of Barrow Street Press. She teaches literature and poetry writing at New School University, NY.

WENDY TAYLOR CARLISLE was born in Manhattan but has been an "accidental Texan" for more than a decade. Her book *Reading Berryman to the Dog* was brought out by Jacaranda Press in 2000. In addition to poems, she has written songs and authored a beginner's book on the wines of France and California.

MARTHA CARLSON-BRADLEY was born in Gardner, Massachusetts, and now lives in Hillsboro, New Hampshire. In 2000, Adastra Press published her chapbook *Nest Full of Cries*, a poem sequence based on "Hansel and Gretel."

Her poems have appeared in *New England Review, Beloit Poetry Journal, Calliope,* and several anthologies.

HAYDEN CARRUTH is the author of more than twenty books of poetry, most recently *Doctor Jazz: Poems 1996–2000* (2001), *Scrambled Eggs & Whiskey* (1996), and *Collected Shorter Poems: 1946–1991* (1992), all from Copper Canyon. He has also published several books of essays and edited *The Voice That Is Great Within Us,* a major anthology of 20th century American poetry.

LUCILLE CLIFTON was born in upstate New York. Her many books of poetry include *Blessing the Boats: New and Selected Poems 1988–2000* (BOA, 2000), *The Terrible Stories* (BOA, 1996), *The Book of Light* (Copper Canyon, 1993), and *Quilting: Poems 1987–1990* (BOA, 1991). She is Distinguished Professor of Humanities at St. Mary's College, MD.

WANDA COLEMAN is the author of many books of poetry and prose, including *Mercurochrome: New Poems* (2001); *Bathwater Wine* (1998), winner of the Lenore Marshall Prize; *Hand Dance* (1993); *African Sleeping Sickness: Stories & Poems* (1990); *Imagoes* (1983); and *Mad Dog, Black Lady* (1979). She lives in Los Angeles.

NICOLE COOLEY was raised in New Orleans. Her book of poems, *Resurrection* (LSU, 1996) won the Walt Whitman Award. *Judy Garland, Ginger Love,* a novel, came out in 1998 from Regan Books/HarperCollins. *The Afflicted Girls,* poems about the Salem witch trials, is forthcoming. She is assistant professor at Queens College–The City University of New York.

PETER COOLEY was born in Detroit and is professor of English at Tulane University, New Orleans. His seven books of poetry include *A Place Made of Starlight* (2002), *Sacred Conversations* (1998), and *The Astonished Hours* (1992), all from Carnegie Mellon. He was the poetry editor of *North American Review* from 1970 to 2000.

BARBARA CROOKER was born in Cold Spring, New York. She has published nine chapbooks, most recently *Ordinary Life* (ByLine, 2001) and *The White Poems* (Barnwood, 2001). Her poems have appeared in many publications such as *Boomer Girls, Thirteen Ways of Looking at a Poem,* and *Worlds in Our Words: An Anthology of Contemporary American Women Writers.*

ENID DAME lives in New York City and High Falls, NY. Her books include *Anything You Don't See* (West End, 1992), *Lilith and Her Demons* (Cross-Cultural Communications, 1989), and *Jerusalem Syndrome* (Three Mile Harbor, 2003). She is coeditor of *Home Planet News* and of *Bridges,* a Jewish feminist magazine, and she teaches at New Jersey Institute of Technology.

MARK DeFOE is the author of *Bringing Home Breakfast* (Black Willow, 1983), *Palmate* (Pringle Tree, 1988), *Air* (Green Tower, 1998), and *Aviary* (Pringle Tree, 2001), and his poems have appeared in numerous magazines, anthologies, and textbooks. He lives in Buckhannon, WV, and is professor of English at West Virginia Wesleyan College.

ANNA DENISE was born in Livermore, California, and now lives in Davis. She received her MLS from San Jose State and currently works as a children's librarian. She is also a storyteller and is at work on a collection of fairy-tale poems.

SHARON DOLIN was born in Brooklyn. Her poetry collections include *Heart Work* (Sheep Meadow, 1995), *Serious Pink* (Marsh Hawk, 2003), and *Realm of the Possible* (forthcoming, 2004). She teaches poetry at the Unterberg Poetry Center of the 92nd Street Y and is coordinator and co-judge of the Center for Book Arts Annual Letterpress Poetry Chapbook Competition.

MOYRA DONALDSON was born in County Down, N. Ireland. Her books are *Kissing Ghosts* (Lapwing, 1995), *Snakeskin Stilettos* (Lagan, 1998; reissued in US by CavanKerry, 2002), and *Beneath the Ice* (Lagan, 2001). She lives in Newtownards, N. Ireland, and has been employed in welfare and education work with young people for two decades.

CAROL ANN DUFFY was born in Glasgow, Scotland. Her books include *The World's Wife* (1999), *Mean Time* (1993), which won the Whitbread and Forward prizes, *The Other Country* (1990), *Selling Manhattan* (1987), and *Standing Female Nude* (1985). She currently lives in Manchester, England.

DENISE DUHAMEL was born in Woonsocket, Rhode Island. She has published several collections of poetry, most recently *The Star-Spangled Banner* (Southern Illinois, 1999) and *Queen for a Day: Selected and New Poems* (Pittsburgh, 2001). She is an assistant professor at Florida International University in Miami.

RUSSELL EDSON grew up in Connecticut where he still lives. He is a recognized master of the prose poem form, and his many books include *The Tormented Mirror* (Pittsburgh, 2001), *The Tunnel: Selected Poems* (FIELD/Oberlin, 1994), *The Wounded Breakfast* (Wesleyan, 1985), *The Intuitive Journey* (Harper & Row, 1976), and *The Clam Theater* (Wesleyan, 1973).

ELAINE EQUI has published several books of poetry including *Surface Tension* (1990); *Decoy* (1994); *Voice-Over* (1999), winner of the San Francisco State Poetry Award; and *The Cloud of Knowable Things* (2003), all from Coffee House Press. A Chicago native, she now lives in Manhattan and teaches at New York University and in the graduate program at City College.

ANNIE FINCH is the author of two books of poetry, *Eve* (Story Line, 1997) and *Brutal Flowers* (Story Line, 2002). She has also written or edited five books on poetry, including *A Formal Feeling Comes*, *The Ghost of Meter*, and *An Exaltation of Forms: Contemporary Poets Celebrate the Diversity of Their Art*. She teaches at Miami University of Ohio and lives in Cincinnati and Maine.

DONALD FINKEL was born in New York City. His numerous books of poetry include *The Clothing's New Emperor* (1958), *A Joyful Noise* (1966), *What Manner of Beast* (1981), *Selected Shorter Poems* (1980), *The Detachable Man* (1984), and most recently *A Question of Seeing* (Arkansas, 1998). He lives in St. Louis, Missouri.

ALICE FRIMAN was born in New York City and is professor emerita of English and creative writing at the University of Indianapolis. She is the author of seven poetry collections including *Inverted Fire* (BkMk Press, 1997) and *Zoo* (Arkansas, 1999), which won the Ezra Pound Poetry Award.

NEIL GAIMAN is a British author who has written in many genres including graphic novels, comic books, screenplays, and fantasy. Among his works are

Outrageous Tales of the Old Testament (1987); the *Sandman* series of graphic novels (1991–1996); the teleplay *Neverwhere* for the BBC, subsequently published as a novel in 1998; and *Stardust* (1999).

AMY GERSTLER writes fiction, art reviews, journalism, and poetry from her home in Los Angeles. Her poetry books include *Medicine* (Penguin, 2000), *Crown of Weeds* (Penguin, 1997), *Nerve Storm* (Penguin, 1993), and *Bitter Angel* (North Point, 1990), winner of the National Book Critics Circle Award for Poetry.

SANDRA M. GILBERT, Professor of English at the University of California, Davis, has published six collections of poetry, most recently *Kissing the Bread: New and Selected Poems 1969–1999* (Norton, 2000) and *Ghost Volcano* (Norton, 1995); a memoir, *Wrongful Death* (1995); and numerous volumes of criticism, some coauthored with Susan Gubar.

LOUISE GLÜCK has written nine books of poetry, most recently *The Seven Ages* (2001), *Vita Nova* (1999), and *Meadowlands* (1996). Her book of prose, *Proofs and Theories: Essays on Poetry* was issued in 1994. Born in New York City, she grew up on Long Island and now lives in Cambridge, MA.

RIGOBERTO GONZÁLEZ was born in Bakersfield, California, and spent much of his childhood in Michoacán, Mexico. He is author of *So Often the Pitcher Goes to Water Until It Breaks* (Illinois, 1999), selected by Ai for the National Poetry Series. His work appears in several anthologies including *American Poetry: Next Generation*. He lives in Brooklyn.

ALICE WIRTH GRAY grew up in Chicago, where Langston Hughes was her first poetry teacher. Her poem "On a 19th Century Lithograph of Red Riding Hood by the Artist J. H." from her book *What the Poor Eat* (Cleveland State, 1993), was set to music by composer Tom Cipullo as part of a song cycle of her poems that has been performed several times in US cities and in Japan.

DEBORA GREGER is the author of several poetry books: *The 1002nd Night* (1990), *And* (1986), *Movable Islands* (1980), all from Princeton; *Off-season at the Edge of the World* (Illinois, 1994); *Desert Fathers, Uranium Daughters* (Penguin, 1996), and *God* (Penguin, 2001). She is a professor at the University of Florida.

R. S. GWYNN was born in Eden, North Carolina. He is author of *No Word of Farewell: Selected Poems 1970–2000* (Story Line, 2001) and editor of two volumes of the *Dictionary of Literary Biography* and the essay anthology *New Expansive Poetry: Theory, Criticism, History*, among other books. He is University Professor of English at Lamar University, Texas.

PAMELA WHITE HADAS was born in Holland, Michigan. Her several poetry books include *Designing Women* (1979), *Beside Herself: Pocahontas to Patty Hearst* (1983), and *Self-Evidence: A Selection of Verse, 1977–1997* (TriQuarterly, 1998). She also authored a book of criticism, *Marianne Moore: Poet of Affection*.

RACHEL HADAS is the author of fifteen books of poetry, prose, and translations, including *Merrill, Cavafy, Poems, and Dreams* (Michigan, 2000), *Indelible* (Wesleyan, 2001), and *Halfway Down the Hall: New and Selected Poems* (Wesleyan, 1998). She is a professor of English at Rutgers University and has also led writing workshops at the Gay Men's Health Alliance in New York.

KIMIKO HAHN is the author of six collections of poetry: *The Artist's Daughter* (Norton, 2002), *Mosquito and Ant* (Norton, 1999), *Volatile* (Hanging Loose, 1999), *The Unbearable Heart* (Kaya, 1995), *Earshot* (Hanging Loose, 1992), and *Air Pocket* (Hanging Loose, 1989). She is a professor at Queens College/CUNY and lives in New York.

BARBARA HAMBY is the author of *The Alphabet of Desire* (New York University Press, 1999), and *Delirium* (North Texas, 1995), and her work also appeared in *The Best American Poetry 2000*. She teaches in the creative writing program at Florida State in Tallahassee.

SARA HENDERSON HAY (1906–1987) won the 1951 Edna St. Vincent Millay Award for *The Delicate Balance* and the Pegasus Award for *The Stone and The Shell* (1961). Other titles include her first book of poems, *Field of Honor* (1933), *A Footing on the Earth: New and Selected Poems* (1966), and the classic fairy-tale collection *Story Hour* (1963).

ESSEX HEMPHILL (1957–1995) was born in Chicago and raised in Washington, DC. He was the editor of *Brother to Brother: New Writings by Black Gay Men* (1991). His work appeared in several anthologies including *In the Life* and *Life Sentences: Writers, Artists and AIDS,* as well as in his collection *Ceremonies: Prose and Poetry* (Plume/Penguin, 1992).

DOROTHY HEWETT (1923–2002) was born in Perth, Western Australia, but spent much of her adult life in Sydney. She published a dozen collections of poetry as well as novels, an autobiography, and many plays. A comprehensive volume of her poetry, *Dorothy Hewett: Collected Poems,* came out from Fremantle Arts Centre Press in 1996.

EMILY HIESTAND is a poet, visual artist, essayist, and travel writer. Her books include *Green the Witch-Hazel Wood* (Graywolf, 1989), *The Very Rich Hours: Travels in Orkney, Belize, the Everglades, and Greece,* and *Angela, the Upside-Down Girl and Other Domestic Travels* (both from Beacon).

BRENDA HILLMAN is the author of several books of poetry including *Cascadia* (2002), *Loose Sugar* (1997), *Bright Existence* (1993), *Death Tractates* (1992), *Fortress* (1989), and *White Dress* (1985), all published by Wesleyan University Press. She lives in Kensington, California.

MARIE HOWE is the author of *What the Living Do* (Norton, 1997) and *The Good Thief* (Persea, 1988) and the coeditor, with Michael Klein, of the anthology *In the Company of My Solitude: American Writing from the AIDS Pandemic* (Persea, 1994). She teaches in the writing program at Sarah Lawrence College, NY.

RANDALL JARRELL (1914–1965) was a noted critic and poet whose books include *Losses, Selected Poems, The Woman at the Washington Zoo, The Lost World, Poetry and the Age,* and *Sad Heart at the Supermarket. The Complete Poems* was issued by Farrar, Straus & Giroux in 1969.

KATHLEEN JESME lives near St. Paul, Minnesota, and works as a freelance training consultant. Her poems have appeared in several journals including *Shenandoah, Prairie Schooner,* and *Great River Review.* Her first collection, *Fire Eater,* will be published in 2003 by Tampa University Press.

MEG KEARNEY is the Associate Director of the National Book Foundation and lives in New York City. Her first book of poems, *An Unkindness of Ravens,* came out from BOA Editions, Ltd. in 2001.

GALWAY KINNELL was born in Providence, Rhode Island. His numerous volumes of poetry include *A New Selected Poems* (Houghton Mifflin, 2000), *Imperfect Thirst* (HM, 1994), *When One Has Lived a Long Time Alone* (HM, 1990), and *Selected Poems* (HM, 1980), which won the Pulitzer Prize.

RON KOERTGE, born in Olney, Illinois, is the author of *Geography of the Forehead* (Arkansas, 2000), *Making Love to Roget's Wife: Poems New and Selected* (Arkansas, 1997), and several books for children and young adults, including *Confess-O-Rama* and *The Heart of the City.* He recently retired from Pasadena City College after 37 years of teaching.

YUSEF KOMUNYAKAA was born in Bogalusa, Louisiana. His many volumes of poetry include *Pleasure Dome: New & Collected Poems, 1975–1999* (Wesleyan, 2001), *Talking Dirty to the Gods* (Farrar, Straus & Giroux, 2000), and the Pulitzer Prize-winning *Neon Vernacular* (Wesleyan, 1993). He is a professor at Princeton University and lives in New York.

MAXINE KUMIN was born in Philadelphia and now lives in New Hampshire. She is the author of *The Long Marriage* (Norton, 2001), *Selected Poems: 1960–1990* (Norton, 1997), *Connecting the Dots* (1996), *Looking for Luck* (1992), and many other poetry collections. A memoir, *Inside the Halo and Beyond: The Anatomy of a Recovery* was published in 2000 by Norton.

DENISE LEVERTOV (1923–1997) was born and raised in England and came to the US in 1948. Her books of poetry cover six decades and include *The Double Image* (1946), *Here and Now* (1957), *O Taste and See* (1964), *The Freeing of the Dust* (1975), *Breathing the Water* (1987), and *Sands of the Well* (1996). Her essays are collected in *The Poet in the World* and *Light Up the Cave.*

ELLINE LIPKIN, born in New Jersey, grew up in North Miami Beach, Florida. She is currently completing her doctorate in Creative Writing and Literature at the University of Houston. She teaches creative writing for Houston's Writers in the Schools and has worked as a freelance editor and writer in New York and Paris.

RACHEL LODEN was born in Washington, DC, and currently lives in Palo Alto, California. Her collection of poems, *Hotel Imperium* (2000), was winner of the Contemporary Poetry Series of the University of Georgia Press. Her poems have appeared in numerous journals and anthologies including *Pushcart Prize XXVI.*

AMY LOWELL (1874–1925) was born in Brookline, Massachusetts. Her first book of poetry, *A Dome of Many-Coloured Glass,* appeared in 1912. Other books include *Men, Women and Ghosts, Pictures of the Floating World,* and the Pulitzer prize-winning *What's O Clock* (1925). She also wrote a biography of John Keats. Her poems are collected in *Complete Poetical Works of Amy Lowell* (Houghton Mifflin, 1955, 1978).

KATHARYN HOWD MACHAN is associate professor of writing and women's studies at Ithaca College, NY, and she serves as Director of the Feminist Women's Writing Workshops. She is author of numerous published collections, most recently *Skyros* (Foothills Publishing, 2001) and *Delilah's Veils* (Sometimes Y Publications, 1999).

CHARLES MARTIN is a poet and translator and a professor at Queensborough Community College. His books of poems include *Starting from Sleep: New and Selected Poems* (Overlook Press, 2002), *Steal the Bacon*, and *What the Darkness Proposes* (both Johns Hopkins University Press).

JANET McADAMS was born in Louisiana and is currently Robert P. Hubbard Professor of Poetry at Kenyon College. Her book *The Island of Lost Luggage* (Arizona, 2000) won an American Book Award, and her poems and criticism have appeared widely in *TriQuarterly, North American Review,* and other journals, and in the anthologies *Outsiders* and *The Year's Best Fantasy and Horror.*

SUSAN MITCHELL grew up in New York City. Her books of poetry are *The Water Inside the Water* (1983), *Rapture* (1992), and *Erotikon* (2000), all available from HarperCollins. She holds the Mary Blossom Lee Endowed Chair in Creative Writing at Florida Atlantic University.

JEAN MONAHAN has published two poetry books: *Hands* (Anhinga, 1992) and *Believe It or Not* (Orchises, 1998), and her work appears in the anthologies *Orpheus & Company* and *And What Rough Beast: Poems at the End of the Century.* Born in Cheshire, Connecticut, she lives in Salem, Massachusetts, and is Senior Creative Director at AGENCY.COM: Boston.

MARTIN MOONEY was born in Belfast, N. Ireland, and grew up in Newtownards, County Down. His first collection, *Grub,* came out from Blackstaff Press in 1993; CavanKerry Press brought out a US edition in 2002. His second collection is *Rasputin and His Children* (Blackwater Press, 2000). He lives in Carrickfergus, N. Ireland.

ROBIN MORGAN, writer, editor, and activist, is the author of several books including *A Hot January: Poems 1996–1999* (Norton, 2001), and *Upstairs in the Garden: Poems Selected and New, 1968–1988* (Norton, 1990). She was editor-in-chief of *Ms. Magazine* and also edited the classic anthologies, *Sisterhood Is Powerful* and *Sisterhood Is Global.*

THYLIAS MOSS was born in Cleveland, Ohio. She is the author of several poetry books, including *Last Chance for the Tarzan Holler* (Persea, 1998), *Small Congregations: New and Selected Poems* (Ecco, 1992), *Rainbow Remnants in Rock Bottom Ghetto Sky* (Persea, 1991), and *At Redbones* (Cleveland State, 1990), as well as a memoir.

LISEL MUELLER was born in Hamburg, Germany. She won the Pulitzer Prize for *Alive Together: New and Selected Poems* (LSU, 1996). Her many other books of poetry include *Waving from Shore* (LSU, 1989); *Second Language* (LSU, 1986); and *The Need to Hold Still* (LSU, 1980). She lives in Chicago.

VALERY NASH is the author of *The Narrows* (Cleveland State, 1980), and *October Swimmer* (Folly Cove Press, 2001). Born in New York City, she currently lives and teaches in Rockport, Massachusetts.

JAMES NOLAN, poet and translator, was born in New Orleans. He is the author of *Why I Live in the Forest* (1974), *What Moves Is Not the Wind* (1979), and *Poet Chief: The Native American Poetics of Walt Whitman and Pablo Neruda* (1994).

GREGORY ORR was born in Albany, New York, and now lives in Charlottesville where he teaches at the University of Virginia. The most recent of his seven volumes of poetry are *The Caged Owl: New and Selected Poems* (Copper Canyon, 2002), *City of Salt* (Pittsburgh, 1995), and *New and Selected Poems* (Wesleyan, 1988).

SUE OWEN is the author of three poetry collections, *Nursery Rhymes for the Dead* (Ithaca House, 1980), *The Book of Winter* (Ohio State, 1988), and *My Doomsday Sampler* (LSU, 1999). She is Poet-in-Residence at Louisiana State University and lives in Baton Rouge.

MARLENE JOYCE PEARSON is a writer of poetry and fiction and a photographer. She is the author of the poetry collection *A Fine Day for a Middle-Class Marriage* (Red Hen, 1996), and teaches writing and literature at California State University, both Northridge and Los Angeles.

ANNA RABINOWITZ is the author of two books of poetry, *At the Site of Inside Out* (Massachusetts, 1997), which won the Juniper Prize, and *Darkling* (Tupelo Press, 2001). Since 1992 she has been editor and publisher of *American Letters & Commentary*. She lives in Manhattan.

ALASTAIR REID was born in Scotland and has lived in Spain, Greece, Morocco, and many other places. He was appointed staff writer at the *New Yorker* in 1959. His books include *Weathering: Poems and Translations* (1978) and *An Alastair Reid Reader: Selected Prose and Poetry* (1994). He is also a noted translator of Pablo Neruda and Jorge Luis Borges, among others.

MARGARET ROCKWELL was born in Bridgeton, New Jersey, and now resides in Bath, Maine. Her work has appeared in *The Saturday Review, The Christian Science Monitor, Voices,* and other journals and in the anthologies *Japan: Theme and Variations* and *The Diamond Anthology* (Poetry Society of America, 1971).

MARTHA RONK is a professor at Occidental College and an editor of Littoral Books. Her books include *Eyetrouble* (Georgia, 1998), *State of Mind* (Sun & Moon, 1995), *Desert Geometries* (Littoral Books, 1993), and *Desire in L.A.: Poems* (Georgia, 1990).

MURIEL RUKEYSER (1913–1980) was born in New York City. Her first book, *Theory of Flight* (1935), was a Yale Younger Poets winner. Her other books of poetry include *The Gates* (1976), *Breaking Open* (1973), *The Speed of Darkness* (1968), and *Out of Silence: Selected Poems* (1992). Among her books of prose is the recently reissued classic *The Life of Poetry* (Paris Press, 1996), first published in 1949.

NATASHA SAJÉ teaches at Westminster College in Salt Lake City, Utah, and also in the Vermont College MFA program. She is the author of *Red Under the Skin* (Pittsburgh, 1994). Her poems, essays, and reviews have appeared in *New Republic, Gettysburg Review, Parnassus, Kenyon Review,* and elsewhere.

TIM SEIBLES was born and raised in Philadelphia. He has published five collections of poems: *Body Moves* (1988), *Hurdy-Gurdy* (1992), *Kerosene* (1995), *Ten Miles an Hour* (1998), and most recently *Hammerlock* (Cleveland State, 1999). His work appears in several anthologies including *New American Poets in the 90s*. He teaches at Old Dominion University.

ANNE SEXTON (1928–1974) was born in Newton, Massachusetts. *Transformations,* her collection of poems based on fairy tales, was published in 1971. That book, along with her other eight collections of poetry, can be found in *The Complete Poems*, which was issued by Houghton Mifflin in 1981.

ANNE SHELDON was born in Washington, DC. She is the author of *Hero-surfing* (Washington Writers' Publishing House, 2002) and a chapbook *Lancastrian Letters* (Word Works, 1997). She is a poet-in-the-schools, working through the Maryland State Arts Council, and teaches storytelling at the library school of University of Maryland.

JANE SHORE is the author of the poetry collections *Happy Family* (Picador, 1999), *Music Minus One* (Picador, 1996), *The Minute Hand* (Massachusetts, 1987), and *Eye Level* (Massachusetts, 1977). She lives in Washington, DC, and Vermont.

PENELOPE SHUTTLE, born in Middlesex, England, now lives in Cornwall. Her poetry books are *The Orchard Upstairs* (1980), *The Child-Stealer* (1983), *The Lion from Rio* (1986), *Adventures with My Horse* (1988), *Taxing the Rain* (1992), *Building a City for Jamie* (1996), and *Selected Poems* (1998), all from Oxford University Press; and *A Leaf Out of His Book* from Carcanet, 1999.

HENRY SLOSS was born and raised in San Francisco and environs. He spent several years in Italy, and his book about his time there, *The Threshold of the New*, appeared from University of South Carolina Press in 1997. He now lives and teaches in Maryland.

STEVIE SMITH (1902–1971) was born Florence Margaret Smith in Hull, England. For 30 years she worked for a publisher in London; she also did work for the BBC. She began publishing poems in the 1930s, often with her own illustrations, and went on to write three novels and eight volumes of poetry. Her life was the subject of Hugh Whitemore's play *Stevie* and the subsequent 1978 film.

LAURENCE SNYDAL, born in Minot, North Dakota, is a poet, musician, and retired teacher. His poetry has appeared in several journals including *Columbia, Cape Rock, Lyric,* and *Gulf Stream.* He has also published two nonfiction books, which are guides for young fathers.

LISA RUSS SPAAR was born in Elizabeth, New Jersey. She is the author of *Glass Town* (Red Hen, 1999) and the editor of the anthology *Acquainted with the Night: Insomnia Poems* (Columbia, 1999). She directs the writing program at the University of Virginia and lives in Charlottesville.

ELIZABETH SPIRES was born in Lancaster, Ohio, and currently lives in Maryland, where she teaches at Goucher College. Her books of poetry include *Globe* (Wesleyan, 1981), *Swan's Island* (Henry Holt, 1985), *Annonciade* (Penguin, 1989), *Worldling* (Norton, 1995), and *Now the Green Blade Rises* (Norton, 2002); she has also written several children's books.

ANN STANFORD (1916–1987) was a poet, editor, translator, and scholar whose publications include *The Weathercock* (1966), *The Descent* (1970), *In Mediterranean Air* (1977), and a critical book *Anne Bradstreet: The Worldly Puritan*. She edited the anthology *The Women Poets in English. Holding Our Own: The Selected Poems of Ann Stanford*, edited by David Trinidad and Maxine Scates, was issued by Copper Canyon Press in 2001.

MAURA STANTON is the author of several books of fiction as well as poetry. Among her poetry collections are *Glacier Wine* (Carnegie Mellon, 2001), *Life Among the Trolls* (Carnegie Mellon, 1997), *Tales of the Supernatural* (Godine,

1988), and her first book, *Snow on Snow,* which won the Yale Younger Poets Prize in 1975.

GWEN STRAUS, who writes both fiction and poetry, was born in Haiti. Her book of fairy-tale poems, *Trail of Stones,* with illustrations by Anthony Browne, was published in 1989 by Knopf. Her work has also appeared in *Frank* and *The Year's Best Fantasy and Horror.*

ALLEN TATE (1899–1979) was born in Winchester, Kentucky. His poetry is collected in *The Swimmers and Other Selected Poems* (Scribners, 1970) and *Collected Poems 1919–1976* (Farrar, Straus & Giroux, 1977). In addition to poetry, he published a novel, biographies, and influential books of criticism. Intercollegiate Studies Institute issued *Essays of Four Decades* in 1999.

MARIA TERRONE, a lifelong resident of New York City, works in public relations. Her first book of poetry, *The Bodies We Were Loaned,* was published in 2002 by The Word Works. Her work also appears in the anthology *The Milk of Almonds: Italian American Women Write on Food and Culture.*

DIANE THIEL is the author of a poetry collection, *Echolocations* (Story Line, 2000), and a writer's guide, *Writing Your Rhythm: Using Nature, Culture, Form & Myth* (Story Line, 2001). She was a Fulbright Scholar for 2001–2002 and spent the year in Odessa. She is currently assistant professor at the University of New Mexico.

JOYCE THOMAS is a professor of English at Castleton State College, Vermont. She is author of *Inside the Wolf's Belly: Aspects of the Fairy Tale* (Sheffield Academic Press, 1989) and a poetry collection *Skins* (Fithian, 2001). Her work appears in *Orpheus & Company: Contemporary Poems of Greek Mythology,* and other publications.

SUSAN THOMAS was born in New York City. Her work has appeared widely in magazines and anthologies; she won the Editor's Prize from the *Spoon River Poetry Review* and the *New York Stories* Fiction Contest. Among her other work in the arts, she has led workshops in fiction, poetry, and mythology for students throughout Vermont, where she now lives.

DAVID TRINIDAD is the author of *Plasticville* (Turtle Point Press, 2000), *Answer Song* (High Risk Books, 1994), *Hand Over Heart* (Amethyst Press, 1991), *November* (Hanuman Books, 1987), and *Pavane* (Sherwood Press, 1981). Originally from Los Angeles, he currently lives in Chicago and teaches at Columbia College.

LEE UPTON was born in St. Johns, Michigan. The most recent of her four books of poetry are *Civilian Histories* (Georgia, 2000) and *Approximate Darling* (Georgia, 1996). Her third book of criticism, *The Muse of Abandonment,* was published by Bucknell University Press in 1998. She is professor of English and writer-in-residence at Lafayette College.

MONA VAN DUYN was born in Waterloo, Iowa, and now lives in St. Louis, Missouri. Her many books of poetry include *Valentines to the Wide World* (1959); *Bedtime Stories* (1972); *Near Changes* (1990), a Pulitzer Prize winner; *Firefall* (1993); and *If It Be Not I: Collected Poems 1959–1982* (Knopf, 1993). She was named Poet Laureate in 1992.

ELLEN BRYANT VOIGT was born in Danville, Virginia. She is the author of several poetry books including *Claiming Kin* (1976), *The Forces of Plenty* (1983), *The Lotus Flowers* (1987), *Two Trees* (1992), *Kyrie* (1995), and *Shadow of Heaven* (Norton, 2001). Her book of essays, *The Flexible Lyric,* was published by University of Georgia Press in 1999.

JEFF WALT is the author of the poetry collection *The Danger in Everything* (Mad River Books, 2000). His work has also been included in the anthologies *Intimate Kisses: The Poetry of Sexual Pleasure* and *Touched by Eros.* He currently lives in Hawaii.

ESTHA WEINER, born in Portland, Maine, now lives in New York City. Her work has appeared in the anthology *Summer Shade: A Collection of Modern Poetry* and in several journals including *New Republic, Lit,* and *Barrow Street.* She is on the faculty at Marymount Manhattan College and The City College of New York, where she directs the Humanities Film Series.

INGRID WENDT lives in Eugene, Oregon. Her poetry books include *Moving the House* (BOA, 1979) and *Singing the Mozart Requiem* (Breitenbush, 1987). She has served on the writing faculty of Antioch University and was a Senior Fulbright Professor at the University of Frankfurt/Main, Germany. For over 20 years she has taught in Arts-in-Education programs in the US and abroad.

SUSAN WHEELER is author of three books of poetry: *Source Codes* (Salt Publishing, 2001), *Smokes* (Four Way Books, 1998), and *Bag 'o' Diamonds* (Georgia, 1993). She is on the faculty of the MFA program at The New School and has also taught at the University of Iowa, Princeton, and New York University. Born in Pittsburgh, she has lived in Manhattan for several years.

TERRI WINDLING has coedited, with Ellen Datlow, nine anthologies of fairy-tale fiction, fifteen annual volumes of *Year's Best Fantasy & Horror,* and many other collections. Her poetry has appeared in *The Armless Maiden* and Jane Yolen's *Xanadu* series, and she is also author of the mythic novel, *The Wood Wife* (1996 Mythopoeic Award). She lives in Tucson, Arizona, and Devon, England.

JANE YOLEN is a poet, playwright, novelist, editor, and writer of children's books. Her more than 250 titles include *The Devil's Arithmetic* (1998), *Briar Rose* (1992), *Child of Faerie* (1996), *The Girl in the Golden Bower* (1995), and *Sleeping Ugly* (1981), to name a few. She also edited *Favorite Folktales from Around the World* (1986).

ACKNOWLEDGMENTS

Authors retain the copyright for their individual poems unless indicated. Grateful acknowledgment is given to the following for permission to include the work in this anthology:

Agha Shahid Ali: "An Interview with Red Riding Hood, Now No Longer Little," "The Wolf's Postscript to 'Little Red Riding Hood'," and "Hansel's Game" from *A Walk Through the Yellow Pages* (Sun/Gemini Press, 1987), © 1987 by Agha Shahid Ali. Reprinted with permission of the Agha Shahid Ali Literary Trust.

Julia Alvarez: "Against Cinderella" from *Homecoming*, © 1984, 1996 by Julia Alvarez. Published by Plume, an imprint of Dutton Signet, a division of Penguin Books USA, Inc.; originally published by Grove Press. Reprinted with permission of Susan Bergholz Literary Services, New York. All rights reserved.

Margaret Atwood: "Girl Without Hands" from *Morning in the Burned House*, © 1995 by Margaret Atwood. Reprinted with permission of Houghton Mifflin Company. All rights reserved. "The Robber Bridegroom" from *Selected Poems II: Poems Selected and New 1976–1986*, © 1987 by Margaret Atwood. Reprinted with permission of Houghton Mifflin Company. All rights reserved.

Mary Jo Bang: "Gretel" from *Apology for Want* (Middlebury College Press), © 1997 by Mary Jo Bang. Reprinted with permission of the University Press of New England.

Carol Jane Bangs: "The Wicked Witch" from *The Bones of the Earth*, © 1983 by Carol Jane Bangs. Reprinted with permission of New Directions Publishing Corporation.

Aliki Barnstone: "Fairy Tale" from *Madly in Love,* © 1997 by Aliki Barnstone. Reprinted with permission of Carnegie Mellon University Press.

Dorothy Barresi: "Cinderella and Lazarus, Part II" from *All of the Above,* © 1991 by Dorothy Barresi. Reprinted with the permission of Beacon Press, Boston.

Jeanne Marie Beaumont: "Hotel Grimm" first appeared in *Rattapallax #6*, reprinted by permission of the author.

Erin Belieu: "Rose Red" from *Infanta*, © 1995 by Erin Belieu. Reprinted by permission of Copper Canyon Press, P.O. Box 271, Port Townsend, WA 98368.

Bruce Bennett: "The Skeptical Prince," "Straw Into Gold," and "The True Story of Snow White" appeared in *Navigating the Distances: Poems New and Selected* (Orchises Press, 1999), © 1999 by Bruce Bennett, reprinted by permission of the author.

Olga Broumas: "Cinderella," "Rapunzel," and "Little Red Riding Hood" from *Beginning with O*, © 1977 by Olga Broumas. Reprinted by permission of Yale University Press.

Andrea Hollander Budy: "Asleep in the Forest," "Gretel," and "Snow White" from *House Without a Dreamer*, © 1993 by Andrea Hollander Budy. Reprinted with permission of Story Line Press.

Emma Bull: "The Stepsister's Story" first appeared in *The Armless Maiden and Other Tales for Childhood's Survivors*, edited by Terri Windling (Tor Books, 1995), © 1995 by Emma Bull. Used by permission of the author.

Regie Cabico: "Hansel Tells Gretel of the Witch" appeared in *Columbia #29* and *Red Brick Review #5*, © 1997 by Regie Cabico, reprinted by permission of the author.

Mike Carlin: "Anaconda Mining Makes the Seven Dwarfs an Offer" is used by permission of the author.

Patricia Carlin: "The Stepmother Arrives," © 2002 by Patricia Carlin, used by permission of the author.

Wendy Taylor Carlisle: "Kissing the Frog" appeared in *Reading Berryman to the Dog* (Jacaranda Press, 2000), © 2000 by Wendy Taylor Carlisle, reprinted by permission of the author.

Claudia Carlson: "Sleeping Beauty Has Words" and "Rumplestiltskin Keeps Mum" first appeared in *nycBigCityLit.com,* © 2001 by Claudia Carlson. Used by permission of the author.

Martha Carlson-Bradley: "The Maiden Without Hands" first appeared in *Marlboro Review,* no. 6, Summer/Fall 1998, © 1998 by Martha Carlson-Bradley. "Hans My Hedgehog" first appeared in *Marlboro Review*, no. 2, Summer/Fall 1996, © 1996 by Martha Carlson-Bradley. "The White Snake" and "One-Eye, Two-Eyes, Three-Eyes" © 2002 by Martha Carlson-Bradley. All used by permission of the author.

Hayden Carruth: Selections from *The Sleeping Beauty,* © 1990 by Hayden Carruth. Reprinted with permission of Copper Canyon Press, P.O. Box 271, Port Townsend, WA 98368.

Lucille Clifton: "sleeping beauty" from *Blessing the Boats: New and Selected Poems 1988–2000,* © 2000 by Lucille Clifton. Reprinted with permission of BOA Editions, Ltd.

Wanda Coleman: "Sex and Politics in Fairyland" from *Hand Dance,* © 1993 by Wanda Coleman. Reprinted with permission of Black Sparrow Press.

Nicole Cooley: "Snow White" from *Resurrection,* © 1996 by Nicole Cooley. Reprinted with permission of Louisiana State University Press. "Rampion," © 2002 by Nicole Cooley, used by permission of the author.

Peter Cooley: "Nocturne with Witch, Oven, and Two Little Figures" from *A Place Made of Starlight* (Carnegie Mellon University Press, 2002), used by permission of the author.

Barbara Crooker: "Masquerade" first appeared in *The National Storytelling Journal,* 1989. Used by permission of the author.

Enid Dame: "Cinderella," from *Anything You Don't See* (West End Press, 1992), reprinted by permission of the author. "The Social Worker Finds Hansel and Gretel Difficult to Place" appeared as part 4 of "Deconstructing Hansel and Gretel" in *Runes,* no. 1, 2001, reprinted by permission of the author.

Mark DeFoe: "Daughters with Toad" from *Air* (Green Tower Press, 1998), also appeared in *Of Frogs & Toads: Poems and Short Prose Featuring Amphibians,* Jill Carpenter, ed. (Ione Press, 1998), © 1998, 2001 by Mark DeFoe. Used by permission of the author.

Anna Denise: "How to Change a Frog Into a Prince," © by Anna Denise. Used by permission of the author.

Sharon Dolin: "Jealousy" first appeared in *Pequod* and appears in *Serious Pink* (Marsh Hawk Press, 2003), © 2001 by Sharon Dolin, used by permission of the author.

Moyra Donaldson: "Babe in the Woods" appeared in *Snakeskin Stilettos* (Lagan Press, 1998 and CavanKerry Press, 2002) and is reprinted by permission of the author and CavanKerry Press.

Carol Ann Duffy: "Little Red Cap" from *The World's Wife,* © 1999 by Carol Ann Duffy. Reprinted with permission of Faber & Faber, Inc., an affiliate of Farrar, Straus & Giroux, LLC.

Denise Duhamel: "Sleeping Beauty's Dreams" from *How the Sky Fell* (Pearl Editions, 1996), © 1996 by Denise Duhamel, reprinted by permission of the author and Pearl Editions. "The Ugly Stepsister" from *Queen for a Day: Selected and New Poems,* by Denise Duhamel, © 2001. Reprinted by permission of the University of Pittsburgh Press.

Russell Edson: "Cinderella's Life at the Castle" from *The Clam Theater,* © 1973 by Russell Edson and reprinted by permission of Wesleyan University Press.

Elaine Equi: "Further Adventures" first appeared in *Conjunctions: 35,* Fall 2000.

Reprinted by permission of the author. "The Objects in Fairy Tales" is used by permission of the author.

Annie Finch: "To the Nixie of the Mill-Pond," © 2002 by Annie Finch. Used by permission of the author.

Donald Finkel: "The Sleeping Kingdom" and "Sleeping Beauty" from *Simeon* (Atheneum, 1964), © 1964 by Donald Finkel. Reprinted by permission of the author.

Alice Friman: "Rapunzel," "Snow White: The Mirror," and "Snow White: The Prince" from *Reporting from Corinth* (Barnwood Press), © 1984 by Alice Friman. Reprinted by permission of the author.

Neil Gaiman: "Instructions" from *A Wolf at the Door,* edited by Ellen Datlow and Terri Windling (Simon & Schuster, 2000), © 2000 by Neil Gaiman, reprinted with permission of the author.

Amy Gerstler: "Lost in the Forest" from *Nerve Storm,* © 1993 by Amy Gerstler. Used by permission of Penguin, a division of Penguin Group (USA). "Scorched Cinderella" from *Medicine,* © 2000 by Amy Gerstler. Used by permission of Penguin, a division of Penguin Group (USA).

Sandra M. Gilbert: "Landscape: In the Forest" from *Emily's Bread,* © 1984 by Sandra M. Gilbert, reprinted by permission of W. W. Norton & Co., Inc. "The Twelve Dancing Princesses" from *Blood Pressure,* © 1988 by Sandra M. Gilbert, reprinted by permission of W. W. Norton & Co., Inc.

Louise Glück: "Gretel in Darkness" from *The First Four Books of Poems by Louise Glück,* © 1968, 1971,1972, 1973, 1974, 1975, 1976, 1977, 1978, 1979, 1980, 1985, 1995 by Louise Glück. Reprinted with permission of HarperCollins Publishers, Inc.

Rigoberto González: "The Girl with No Hands," is used by permission of the author.

Alice Wirth Gray: "On a 19th Century Lithograph of Red Riding Hood by the Artist J. H." and "Snow White and the Man Sent to Fetch Her Heart" from *What the Poor Eat* (Cleveland State University, 1993), © 1993 by Alice Wirth Gray, reprinted by permission of the author.

Debora Greger: "Briar Rose" from *Off-season at the Edge of the World,* © 1994 by Debora Greger. Reprinted with permission of the author and University of Illinois Press. "Snow White and Rose Red" and "Ever After" from *The 1002nd Night,* © 1990 by Princeton University Press. Reprinted by permission of the publisher.

R. S. Gwynn: "Snow White and the Seven Deadly Sins" from *No Word of Farewell: Selected Poems 1970–2000* (Story Line Press, 2001). Reprinted by permission of Story Line Press.

Pamela White Hadas: "Queen Charming Writes Again" from *Self Evidence: A Selection of Verse 1977–1997* (TriQuarterly Books), © 1998 by Pamela White Hadas. Reprinted with permission of Northwestern University Press.

Rachel Hadas: "The Wolf in the Bed" and "The Sleeping Beauty" from *Halfway Down the Hall,* © 1998 by Rachel Hadas, reprinted by permission of Wesleyan University Press.

Kimiko Hahn: "Fervor" is used by permission of the author.

Barbara Hamby: "Achtung, My Princess, Good Night" from *The Alphabet of Desire* (New York University Press, 1999), © 1999 by Barbara Hamby. Reprinted by permission of the author.

Sara Henderson Hay: "The Witch," "The Sleeper 1," "The Sleeper 2," and "Juvenile Court" from *Story Hour,* © 1961, 1963, 1982 by Sara Henderson Hay, © 1998 by the Board of Trustees of the University of Arkansas Press. Reprinted with the permission of University of Arkansas Press.

Essex Hemphill: "Song for Rapunzel" from *Ceremonies,* © 1992 by Essex Hemphill. Used by permission of Plume, an imprint of Penguin Group (USA) Inc.

Dorothy Hewett: "Grave Fairytale" from *Rapunzel in Suburbia* (Prism Books, 1975) and *Collected Poems,* Fremantle Arts Centre Press, Australia, 1995. Reprinted with permission of the publishers.

Emily Hiestand: "The Old Story" from *Green the Witch-Hazel Wood,* © 1989 by Emily Hiestand. Reprinted with the permission of Graywolf Press, St. Paul, MN.

Sue Owen: "The Poisoned Apple" and "The Glass Coffin" from *The Book of Winter* (Ohio State University Press, 1988), © 1988 by Sue Owen. Reprinted by permission of the author.

Marlene Joyce Pearson: "Twenty Years After" and "This Is a Convalescent Home, Not the Fairy Tale Cottage and Always the Good Father" from *A Fine Day for a Middle Class Marriage,* © 1996 by Marlene Joyce Pearson. Reprinted with the permission of Red Hen Press, Los Angeles, CA.

Anna Rabinowitz: "Beauty Sleeping Now" is used by permission of the author.

Alastair Reid: "A Spell for Sleeping," © by Alastair Reid. Used with the permission of the author.

Margaret Rockwell: "The Twelve Dancing Princesses," © by Margaret R. Finch. Used by permission of the author.

Martha Ronk: "Dock" from *Eyetrouble,* © 1998 by Martha Ronk. Reprinted with permission of University of Georgia Press.

Muriel Rukeyser: "Fable" from *The Gates* (McGraw Hill, 1976), © 1976 by Muriel Rukeyser. Reprinted by permission of International Creative Management, Inc.

Natasha Sajé: "Rampion" from *Red Under the Skin,* © 1994 by Natasha Sajé. Reprinted by permission of the University of Pittsburgh Press.

Tim Seibles: "What Bugs Bunny Said to Red Riding Hood" from *Hammerlock* (Cleveland State University Press, 1999), © 1999 by Tim Seibles. Reprinted by permission of the author.

Anne Sexton: "The Twelve Dancing Princesses" from *Transformations,* © 1971 by Anne Sexton. Reprinted with permission of Houghton Mifflin Company. All rights reserved.

Anne Sheldon: "The Prince Who Woke Briar Rose" first appeared in *Pivot,* #48, 1999, and is reprinted by permission of the author. "Snow White Turns 39" first appeared in *Worlds of Fantasy and Horror,* Winter 1996–97, and is reprinted by permission of the author.

Jane Shore: "The Glass Slipper" from *The Minute Hand,* © 1987 by Jane Shore. Reprinted with the permission of University of Massachusetts Press.

Penelope Shuttle: "Ashputtel" from *The Lion from Rio* (Oxford University Press, 1986), reprinted by permission of Carcanet Press Limited.

Henry Sloss: "Fairy Tales" first appeared in *Paris Review,* Spring 1994, © 1994 by Henry Sloss. Used by permission of the author.

Stevie Smith: "The Frog Prince" from *Collected Poems of Stevie Smith,* © 1972 by Stevie Smith. Reprinted by permission of New Directions Publishing Corporation.

Laurence Snydal: "Grandmother" first appeared in *Columbia: A Journal of Literature and Art* #31, 1999, and was reprinted in *The Year's Best Fantasy & Horror,* 2000, © 1999 by Lawrence Snydal; used by permission of the author.

Lisa Russ Spaar: "Rapunzel's Clock" and "Rapunzel Shorn" from *Glass Town,* © 1999 by Lisa Russ Spaar. Reprinted with the permission of Red Hen Press, Los Angeles, CA.

Elizabeth Spires: "Black Fairy Tale" from *Annonciade,* © 1989 by Elizabeth Spires. Used by permission of Viking Penguin, a division of Penguin Group (USA) Inc.

Ann Stanford: "The Bear" appeared in *The Weathercock* (Viking, 1966), and is reprinted by permission of Rosanna Norton on behalf of the Ann Stanford Estate. "The Sleeping Princess" from *Holding Our Own: The Selected Poems of Ann Stanford,* © 2001 by Rosanna Norton on behalf of the Ann Stanford Estate. Reprinted with the permission of Copper Canyon Press, P. O. Box 271, Port Townsend, WA 98368.

Maura Stanton: "The Fisherman's Wife" and "The Goosegirl" from *Snow on Snow,* © 1975 by Maura Stanton. Reprinted with the permission of Yale University Press.

Gwen Straus: "Cinderella," "Her Shadow," and "The Prince" from *Trail of Stones,* © 1990 by Gwen Straus. Reprinted with permission of Alfred A. Knopf Children's Books, a division of Random House, Inc.

Allen Tate: "The Robber Bridegroom" from *Collected Poems 1919–1976,* © 1977 by Allen

SELECTED BIBLIOGRAPHY

Here are some key references, with an emphasis on poetry and poetry-related resources, that the editors found of use or interest. For a comprehensive bibliography of critical work on the Brothers Grimm and their tales, see the *Oxford Companion to Fairy Tales* listed below.

Books

Bernheimer, Kate, ed. *Mirror, Mirror on the Wall: Women Writers Explore Their Favorite Fairy Tales* (Anchor Books/Doubleday, 1998). Of particular interest, Margaret Atwood's essay on Grimm tales with birds and Joyce Carol Oates' essay, which includes a discussion of Anne Sexton's *Transformations*.

Bettelheim, Bruno. *The Uses of Enchantment: The Meaning and Importance of Fairy Tales* (Vintage, 1977).

Bottigheimer, Ruth B. *Grimms' Bad Girls and Bold Boys: The Moral and Social Vision of the Tales* (Yale, 1987). A scholarly and entertaining look at society reflected in the world of Grimm.

Broumas, Olga. *Beginning with O* (Yale, 1977). Includes a group of seven poems drawing on fairy-tale sources (three are in this anthology), as well as several poems with other mythological references.

Carpenter, Jill, ed. *Of Frogs & Toads: Poems and Short Prose Featuring Amphibians* (Ione Press, 1998). This anthology includes a chapter on frog princes.

Carruth, Hayden. *The Sleeping Beauty* (Copper Canyon, 1990). The book-length sequence from which the three selections on pages 88–90 were chosen. An exquisite and far-reaching meditation in 125 cantos.

Complete Fairy Tales of the Brothers Grimm, The, translated and with an introduction by Jack Zipes (Bantam Books, 1987, 1992). Zipes' translation of the Grimm tales is essential to any fairy-tale lover's library.

Dahl, Roald. *Roald Dahl's Revolting Rhymes*, illustrated by Quentin Blake (Knopf, 1982). Not just for kids, Dahl retells six fairy tales in verse, including Grimm's "Cinderella," "Snow White," and "Little Red Riding Hood." His version of "Hansel and Gretel" is in *Rhyme Stew* (Viking, 1990).

Datlow, Ellen, and Terri Windling, eds. Annual fairy-tale and fantasy anthologies (1993–1999) that included poetry: *Black Thorn, White Rose; Snow White, Blood Red; Ruby Slippers, Golden Tears; Black Swan, White Raven; Silver Birch, Blood Moon; Black Heart, Ivory Bones.* Published in the US by Avon.

Datlow, Ellen, and Terri Windling, eds. *A Wolf at the Door and Other Retold Fairy Tales* (Aladdin, 2001). See especially the long poem "The Seven Stage a Comeback" by Gregory Maguire.

Datlow, Ellen, and Terri Windling, eds. *The Year's Best Fantasy and Horror* (annual, 14 volumes to date, St. Martin's Press, 1988–). This anthology series reprints magical fiction and poems published each year. Windling edits the fantasy half of the book, and her introduction lists fairy-tale poem collections and novelizations.

Duhamel, Denise. *How the Sky Fell* (Pearl Editions, 1996). Fairy-tale inspired poems.

Finkel, Donald. *Simeon* (Atheneum, 1964). Collection contains several fairy-tale related poems, in addition to the two we selected for this anthology.

Hay, Sara Henderson. *Story Hour*. Originally published by Doubleday & Company in 1963 as a collection of 30 fairy-tale sonnets with illustrations by Jim McMullan. Reissued in an expanded edition of 41 poems with different illustrations by University of Arkansas Press in 1998.

Jarrell, Randall. *The Complete Poems* (Farrar, Straus & Giroux, 1969). Several of Jarrell's poems, in addition to the two reprinted in this anthology, draw on or refer to fairy-tale sources including "The Märchen," "The House in the Wood," "A Quilt-Pattern," and "Forest Murmurs," his translation of a poem by Eduard Mörike.

Jarvis, Shawn C., and Jeannine Blackwell, eds and trans. *The Queen's Mirror: Fairy Tales by German Women, 1780–1900* (University of Nebraska, 2001). Among the many gems of this recent anthology are a "freely adapted" dramatic version of Snow White in rhymed couplets and tales by Wilhelm Grimm's daughter-in-law, Gisela von Arnim.

Mieder, Wolfgang, ed. *Disenchantments: An Anthology of Modern Fairy Tale Poetry* (University of Vermont/University Press of New England, 1985). Now out of print, this book is available from UMI Books on Demand.

Ostriker, Alicia. "Thieves of Language: Women Poets and Revisionist Mythology," in *Stealing the Language* (Beacon Press, 1986, Chapter 6). Sexton's *Transformations* is discussed in the context of other myths explored by poets.

Schnackenberg, Gjertrud. *Supernatural Love: Poems 1976–1992* (Farrar, Straus & Giroux, 2000). Contains the notable long poem "Imaginary Prisons," a version of Sleeping Beauty.

Sexton, Anne. *Transformations* (Houghton Mifflin, 1971). Influential and essential book of fairy-tale poems. The entire text can also be found in Sexton's *Complete Poems* (Houghton Mifflin, 1981).

Sitwell, Edith. "The Sleeping Beauty" in *The Collected Poems* (Vanguard Press, 1954), pp 46-108. A long poem, that, although presented in 26 parts, proved resistant to excerpting.

Spaar, Lisa Russ. *Glass Town* (Red Hen Press, 1999). Contains the 10-poem sequence "Rapunzel's Clock," from which we reprinted the two poems on pages 74 and 112.

Straus, Gwen. *The Trail of Stones* (Knopf, 1990). Book-length series of fairy-tale poems with illustrations by Anthony Browne.

Wagoner, David. *Through the Forest: New & Selected Poems* (The Atlantic Monthly Press, 1987). Two longer fairy-tale poems in this collection are well worth looking at: "Sleeping Beauty" and "Prince Charming."

Zipes, Jack. *Fairy Tale as Myth, Myth as Fairy Tale* (University Press of Kentucky, 1994). A lively discussion of fairy-tale origins and fairy tales and contemporary culture. Several sections mention the use of fairy tales by contemporary writers, including poets, and there is also a chapter on Robert Bly's *Iron John*.

Zipes, Jack, ed. *Don't Bet on the Prince: Contemporary Feminist Fairy Tales in North America and England* (Methuen, 1987; reprinted by Routledge, 1989). Includes poetry and prose, along with a selection of feminist literary criticism.

Zipes, Jack, ed. *The Oxford Companion to Fairy Tales* (Oxford University Press, 2000). Indispensable guide, with extensive bibliography of fairy-tale scholarship.

About the Brothers Grimm

Michaelis-Jena, Ruth. *The Brothers Grimm* (Praeger, 1970). Biography notable for its many illustrations and plates.

Peppard, Murray B. *Paths Through the Forest: A Biography of the Brothers Grimm* (Holt, Rinehart, 1971). Focuses on scholarly achievements and public careers of the brothers.

Other Media

Cinderella. Music by Richard Rodgers, book and lyrics by Oscar Hammerstein II. March 31, 1957. A lovely traditional retelling, first developed for television starring Julie Andrews. Best known songs are "In My Own Little Corner," "Impossible," and "Ten Minutes Ago." Subsequent remakes have starred Lesley Ann Warren in 1965 and Brandy in 1997.

Into the Woods. Music and lyrics by Stephen Sondheim, book by James Lapine. First Broadway opening November 5, 1987. This musical blends various fairy tales (including Grimm's Rapunzel, Little Red Riding Hood, and Cinderella) and explores what happens after "Happily Ever After." Sondheim's lyrics redefine traditional fairy tales and spin their metaphors in modern life. "Agony" brilliantly explores the desires of princes after they've found true love. The text of the play is available in book form from Theatre Communications Group, Inc., New York.

Online Resources

The Cinderella Project. www-dept.usm.edu/~engdept/cinderella/cinderella.html, a text and image archive prepared by University of Southern Mississippi graduate students led by Michael N. Salda. This group also maintains the *Little Red Riding Hood Project* at www-dept.usm.edu/~engdept/lrrh/lrrhhome.htm.

The Endicott Studio of Mythic Arts, founded by Terri Windling in 1987, www.endicott-studio.com. Online since 1997. A collection of modern myth and fairy-tale poems in "The Coffeehouse" www.endicott-studio.com/cofehous.html and essays in "The Forum."

The National Geographic website reprints their magazine article "Guardians of the Fairy Tale: The Brothers Grimm," by Thomas O'Neill (pages 102–29, December 1999), at www.nationalgeographic.com/grimm/. The online site features 12 tales based on a 1914 translation, a map of the "Fairy-tale Road" that locates the settings of many of the stories and covers 370 miles (596 kilometers) through Germany, and brief biographies of the brothers.

Rapunzel Project. www.gwu.edu/~folktale/GERM232/rapunzel/fairy.htm, includes tale variations, motifs, feminist interpretations, visual images, and other commentary and links related to Rapunzel.

Snow White Links. http://scils.rutgers.edu/~kvander/swlinks.html, selected by Kay E. Vandergrift, is a great resource for links to information on folklore, fairy tales, and myth, including several web sites about Grimm tales.

The SurLaLune Fairy Tales Website, created by Heidi Anne Heiner in 1999, www.surlalunefairytales.com, includes a wealth of information on classic fairy tales, including the better known Grimm tales; lists modern poetry adaptations and links to a fairy-tale discussion board.

INDEX OF POEMS BY TALE

This index lists only those poems that incorporate or refer to elements of one specific tale. Other poems in the anthology combine elements from several Grimm stories, including tales not listed here, or refer to aspects of the tales in a more general way. The titles are listed by Jack Zipes' translations first, with alternate and popular titles following.

INDEX OF AUTHORS AND TITLES

ABOUT THE EDITORS

JEANNE MARIE BEAUMONT was born and raised in the Philadelphia suburbs. Her first book, *Placebo Effects,* selected by William Matthews for the National Poetry Series, was published by Norton in 1997. *Curious Conduct* is forthcoming from BOA Editions, Ltd. in 2004. For seven years she was coeditor of the literary journal *American Letters & Commentary.* She has taught at the 92nd Street Y in New York, at the Frost Place in Franconia, NH, and at Rutgers University, NJ. She has made her home in Manhattan since 1983.

CLAUDIA CARLSON was born in Indiana and raised in college towns across the United States. She has worked as a cartographer, website designer, and water-colorist. She coauthored *The Bulgarian Americans*, Chelsea House, 1990. Her poems have been published in *Coracle, Heliotrope, Rattapallax, Space & Time, Fantastic Stories,* and *nycBigCityLit.com.* She is a senior book designer at Oxford University Press and lives in Manhattan with her family. She is working on a collection of her fairy-tale poems.

PS 595 .F32 P64 2003

The poets' Grimm

DATE DUE
